Books by Keely Brooke Keith

UNCHARTED
The Land Uncharted
Uncharted Redemption
Uncharted Inheritance
Christmas with the Colburns
Uncharted Hope
Uncharted Journey
Uncharted Destiny
Uncharted Promises
Uncharted Freedom
Uncharted Courage

UNCHARTED BEGINNINGS
Aboard Providence
Above Rubies
All Things Beautiful

D1738741

ABOVE RUBIES

KEELY BROOKE KEITH

Edenbrooke
Press

Cover designed by Najla Qamber Designs
Interior design by Edenbrooke Press
Author photo courtesy of Frank Auer

Printed in the United States of America

ISBN-13: 9781542599276
ISBN-10: 154259927X

For my faithful readers.
Thank you for taking these journeys with me!

CHAPTER ONE

The settlement of Good Springs
Autumn, 1863

Olivia Owens shook a patchwork quilt open with a snap, rustling a flurry of white skippers from their clover flower feasts. She knelt on the blanket's soft center and spread its corners flat over the grass near the settlement's new church building. Indigo embroidery spelled out the names of her parents and siblings on the quilt's yellow trim. Often, she was able to read the cross-stitched letters, but not now. The letters spelled words and the words had meaning. She could stare as long as she liked when this happened, but words would not appear. The monster hid them from her, and she hid the monster from everyone else.

An hourglass shaped shadow moved over Olivia's picnic blanket. Peggy Cotter hovered regally above, wearing perfectly polished boots, crinoline puffed skirts, and honey-hued ringlets shaded by a matching parasol. She smiled at Olivia, and dimples pitted her porcelain cheeks. "You won't believe what I just heard from Frances!"

Olivia squinted from the sun glaring over Peggy's parasol. "Do I want to?"

"Gabriel McIntosh kissed Cecelia Foster."

No, she didn't want to hear that. "Good for her," Olivia mumbled.

"I should think not! Gabe is such a cad. Haven't I told you?"

"Many times. Perhaps you should tell Cecelia."

"No, she will discover it for herself soon enough." Peggy flicked a lace-covered wrist and giggled. "And then there will be a scandal."

Olivia glanced at the church families, who were preparing for the picnic. They were trying to build a Christ-honoring community here. She sent Peggy a pleading look. "Don't spend the afternoon spreading gossip."

"Fine. You might not care what happens in this settlement, but I do." Peggy's skirts swished and crinkled as she walked away with tiny, rapid steps. She slithered across the grass and wedged her fashion plate figure close to her mother. Peggy whispered to her mother and pointed at Cecelia.

No sooner had Olivia looked away and Gabriel McIntosh strutted past her quilt, holding a hammer. Perhaps it had permanently fused to his palm after two years of building in the settlement. His broad-shouldered frame blocked the autumn sunlight as he turned back to her. "That's a big blanket for a girl with no food. Where is the famous Owens family feast this week?"

He almost got a smile out of her. She quelled it in time and resumed smoothing the blanket. "Walter and Alice went with my mother to get the food from our house after the service ended. They should be back soon."

"You must have drawn the long straw today." He grinned, deepening the smile lines on his clean-shaven face. Her mother was right: a handsome man shouldn't be trusted.

"If getting up before dawn to start cooking is the more desirable task, then yes I suppose I did."

Gabe stepped closer. His work-worn boots crunched fallen leaves. "You braided your hair differently."

"No, I didn't." She reached for the braid that had fallen to the front of her pearl-buttoned jacket. He was right. "Oh, I had forgotten."

"I like it." He'd shed the waistcoat and cravat he had worn over his starched blue shirt to the morning service. Now he'd cuffed his sleeves, ready to fix something for someone. He pointed at the blanket with his hammer. "Do you need help with that?"

She raised an eyebrow at his tool and chuckled. "Are you offering to nail my quilt to the ground?"

"No." He laughed with a robust happiness that drew the attention of the others at the after-church gathering. Women paused emptying picnic baskets, and men ceased their masculine conferring long enough to stare.

Olivia cringed. One little joke had escaped her lips, and now she would be the topic of hushed gossip all afternoon. That seemed to be all the parents in the settlement spoke of during social gatherings—which young person would marry whom and when. She hated hearing her name mentioned in those conversations, especially in connection with a cad like Gabriel McIntosh.

Gabe didn't take his eyes off her. That must be the same look he had given Cecelia Foster before he kissed her. She tucked her chin, wishing he would move along. Wasn't it enough that his jocularity had made a spectacle? Did he have to pretend to like looking at her too? If he caught a glimpse of Peggy Cotter, it would certainly divert his attention.

A dozen children, dressed in their Sunday best, were playing on the front steps of the newly dedicated chapel. The wooden heels of their leather lace-up boots clicked on the stone stairs. The girls twirled in their printed cotton dresses with their white stockings gleaming in the sunlight. Two of the boys started swinging from the wooden railing at the top of the steps, and soon all of the boys clamored for a chance to swing from it too.

Tomorrow morning they would be Olivia's first class of students. She cupped her hands around her mouth so her voice would carry across the churchyard. "Please don't play on the railing, boys."

The children continued playing while singing improvised rhymes about pioneers clearing land and digging wells. The boys took turns hanging from the rails, dirtying their trousers more each time they dropped to the ground.

Gabe smirked at Olivia. "They aren't going to obey you with that cheery tone. You will have to speak with authority if you want them to listen."

She took his unsolicited advice and affected her voice with firmness but aimed it at him instead. "Don't you have some hammering to do?" Without waiting for his response, she stood, looked at the children, and tried again. "No hanging from the railing!"

One of the boys lost his grip and tumbled to the ground. He sprang to his feet and popped his suspenders, laughing. Within seconds, the children resumed their rail swinging.

Gabe's mocking gaze inflamed Olivia's threadbare pride. She pretended to ignore him. Finally, he walked to the chapel. He spoke to the children as he passed them on the steps. His words were lost in the wind before they could reach Olivia's ears, but the children immediately dispersed. He glanced back at Olivia and winked before he disappeared into the chapel.

She wished she could follow him inside. He was nice to talk to when he wasn't trying to impress her or flirt. Both rankled, but flirtation only led to disappointment.

Olivia's mother and two of her five siblings trudged across the sandy road to the churchyard, carrying pots of food. Olivia left the quilt to help them. She took one of the pots and followed her mother back to their picnic blanket. Mrs. Mary Owens halted her shiny church shoes at the edge of the quilt in front of the indigo stitches, which now clearly spelled out The Owens Family.

Oh good, the monster was gone.

Mary heaved a breath through thin lips as she lowered a steaming pot to the ground. Alice plunked the basket of bread onto the blanket and started scanning the crowd for the other thirteen-year-olds. Walter towered behind their mother with an armload of tin dishes, awaiting instruction.

Mary tossed the potholders to the quilt and glowered at Walter. "Next time, you carry the meat pot." Her stern voice hadn't lost its sharpness, even after a morning spent in church. "If you want your father and me to treat you like a grown man, then behave like one."

"Yes, ma'am." Walter lowered the dishes to the blanket. The instant his hands were empty, he strode to a group of men near the chapel. Their father greeted Walter with a vigorous pat on the back.

"Sixteen," Mary huffed to no one in particular. "Thinks he knows everything. All he knows is how to crack rocks," she motioned to the meat pot, "and how to hunt with a bow."

"Walter has kept fresh meat on the table since we came to this land." Olivia unwrapped the bread loaf in the basket. "And Father says he will be a fine mason someday."

Mary dismissed the positive words with a toss of her wrist. "If you'd been a boy, it would be you learning your father's trade."

"Then I'm especially thankful to God He made me how I am." Except for the word blindness that crept in unpredictably, but she kept that to herself. "All I want to do is teach school."

"Sometimes I wish all six of you children had been boys." Mary uncovered a dish of baked potatoes and continued unabated. "Maybe then your father would have enough stonecraft workers to be content."

There was no pleasing a frustrated parent. Olivia sighed as she shooed a fly from their food. "You have worked so hard here. We all have, and finally we are seeing the fruit of our labor. The settlement feels more like a real town every day.

"Never mind all of that. I'm not sure what has come over me." Mary rubbed her long neck and stared at the chapel, glassy-eyed. "Before we left America, I enjoyed teaching. But after two years of building and tilling and harvesting... I've lost my verve, especially the energy needed to capture a class's attention. At twenty, you possess it in abundance."

"And tomorrow morning, I'll have a classroom of children eager to learn."

"Let's hope they are eager to learn," Mary smiled, "for your sake."

For a moment Olivia thought she saw the old spark of joy behind her mother's eyes, but it left as quickly as it came. She longed to see it again.

The group of men disbanded, and Walter and their father walked toward the picnic blanket. Olivia's other siblings ran to join them.

Mary glanced at the food and spread her hands. "No milk?"

Olivia shook her head, and a clump of dark hair dropped in front of her eye. It blackened part of her vision. She tucked it into her long braid. "Our cow was dry again this morning. We only have one bottle left in the cold box in the creek. If she doesn't produce tomorrow, there won't be enough for the girls and Richie."

Mary raised her eyebrows as Olivia's young siblings crowded the picnic blanket. She whispered, "There is nothing wrong with the cow. Someone must be milking her at night."

"What?" Olivia began to question, but stopped when her mother shot her a look. She would have to wait until they were alone again to find out why her mother would toss out such an accusation. No one in this community would steal. Maybe someone's calf was getting loose. Yes, that must be what she meant.

Alice glanced between them with unconcealed suspicion, so Olivia tried to distract her sister. She gripped the lid of the meat pot with a potholder. "The roast turned out nicely, did it not?"

As she lifted the lid, the scent of venison and onions rose with the steam. It mixed with the briny breeze coming from the nearby ocean. She inhaled these scents of home and cast her gaze about the settlement of Good Springs.

Reverend Colburn called the group's attention and said the blessing for their meal. His dignified voice projected across the churchyard. Children swarmed the food and filled their plates. Older girls cut meat for their younger siblings, and mothers fed their babies. Chatter carried from one blanket to the next as the settlers relaxed into their afternoon of fellowship. It would be the last after-church picnic until spring.

Once the dessert plates were emptied, youngsters gathered beneath a nearby gray leaf tree to toss horseshoes while adults mingled and children played. Olivia relaxed in the autumn sun's fleeting warmth and stretched her legs along the withering grass.

Across from her, Mrs. Susanna Vestal trailed her eighteen-month-old twins as they toddled through the churchyard. The eldest of the Vestal children, Hannah, usually watched the girls, but she'd just stepped into the outhouse behind the chapel. The twin girls' blond ringlets bounced when they suddenly darted in different directions. One girl chased a dog toward the grove as the other girl ran toward the horseshoe game.

Panic flashed across their mother's exhausted face. Susanna followed one twin toward the grove, so Olivia jumped to her feet and dashed to catch the other girl. A horseshoe flew through the air inches from the toddler's head. Olivia hoisted the little girl from the ground. Iron clanked against iron as the horseshoe hit a stake. She plunked the oblivious child onto her hip and wagged a finger. "No running into horseshoes games, young lady."

Her scold was not understood. She held the tiny girl close, thankful the horseshoe hadn't hit her. The toddler arched her back, wanting down. Olivia tickled her protruding belly. "Until you learn to watch where you're going, I will have to watch out for you, won't I?"

The girl giggled and arched again.

"No, I'm not falling for that game, either." Olivia laughed and carried her across the grass.

Susanna's shoulders hunched as she wrangled the youngest of her brood toward her family's blanket. If anyone needed a relaxing afternoon, it was Susanna Vestal. She blew a strand of sweaty hair off her pale forehead. "Thank you, Olivia. These girls are bent on wearing out their old mother."

Black circles framed Susanna's eyes and had since the twins' harrowing birth, but she wasn't old. Christopher Vestal was in his forties, but Susanna had recently turned thirty-four. Lately, she looked older than the other mothers, even though she was one of the youngest. Perhaps prolonged exhaustion aged a person.

Susanna waved a willowy arm at Mr. Vestal, who was near the road, conversing with other men. "Christopher!" she called out and caught his attention. Both of the twins ran for him, arms outstretched. Susanna sighed and followed the twins to their smiling father.

Mr. Vestal scooped up both girls, one in each arm. Displays of a strong father's affection rarely stirred Olivia, but when they did, a surge of primal desire for a future that could not be left her discontent.

As the Vestals walked away, Olivia stared longer than she intended. They had something she never would, but it shouldn't matter because she didn't want it anyway. At least not like that—six children and tired eyes.

At twenty Olivia's singleness would have qualified her for spinsterhood back in Virginia. But things were different here.

Forming a new society was isolating, but it came with the freedom to forget erstwhile customs. Still, she rather liked the idea of spinsterhood. Her only desire for children was to educate them. Being labeled a spinster teacher would mean she'd achieved her goal.

Both for the children and for herself.

She had waited two long years for the settlement to be built and for the homesteads to be stable enough for families to send their children to school. Between every tedious chore she had scribbled lesson ideas. During sleepless nights, stuck beside snoring siblings in the family's cramped cabin, she had imagined the class's seating arrangement. When she should have been listening to the reverend's sermons, she had planned the weeks of review lessons the students would need after two years without schooling. And she did it all while fighting a monster that often blinded her to the written word—sometimes for seconds, sometimes for the rest of the day.

Now that the elders had finally decided the settlement's formal education could begin, it would all be worthwhile. Tomorrow morning, come storm or sun, Olivia—Miss Owens to her students—would ring the bell for the school at nine o'clock sharp even though there were no desks or chairs yet. If the congregation didn't mind sitting on the chapel's wooden floor while Reverend Colburn delivered a two-hour sermon, surely the children could do the same while she taught, at least until desks were built. She had her first week of lectures memorized, so if the words on the page disappeared while she taught, no one would discover her shortcoming.

Olivia glanced at the chapel. The last of the gray leaf tree lumber piled on the ground outside awaited the carpentry skills of Gabe and his father to build seats and a lectern. As the reverend had made clear in his lengthy, albeit meaningful, dedication prayer this morning, all of it was for the church. Olivia's delight was in knowing four days a week the chapel would be her schoolhouse. Of course the impetuousness of claiming the chapel belonged to anyone but God forced her to keep her sentiment to herself.

Beneath the sounds of the horseshoe game and the laughter and the children singing, the low thuds of Gabe's hammer echoed from inside the chapel. He'd missed the meal. While everyone was outside, socializing and enjoying a day of rest, Gabe was alone inside, working.

Olivia walked back to her family's quilt. She lifted the lid from the meat pot. One lone chunk of venison swam in the lukewarm broth. She forked it onto a plate along with the last baked potato and a heel of fresh bread.

Holding the plate with one hand, she raised the front of her skirt with the other and climbed the stone steps her father and Walter had laid for the chapel only weeks ago. A chunk of stone propped the arched wooden door open. The minty-sharp scent of freshly hewn gray leaf lumber flowed from the narrow sanctuary.

It took a moment for her vision to adjust to the low light in the chapel. Gabe was at the front of the empty room on his knees, driving a nail into a floorboard. His hammer paused as he drew another nail from between his lips, and then he drove it into the wood.

Olivia waited until Gabe finished hammering. "You haven't eaten."

He wiped his forehead with his shirtsleeve and stood. "Did my mother send you?"

She proffered the plate of food. "No."

"Thanks, Liv." A cheeky grin slowly reached his eyes as he accepted the plate. "So you do care about me."

Of course she cared about him. They had known each other their entire lives. His charm couldn't fool her. He might enjoy flirting, but she didn't like to pretend there could ever be anything more between them. She put up both hands in resignation. "I'm leaving."

"No, please stay," Gabe slurred through a mouthful of food. He covered his lips with the back of his hand as he swallowed. "I was kidding. Don't be like that."

"Like what?"

"So easily offended."

"I'm not." When she faced him, his steel blue eyes were studying her. She was glad she'd never fallen in love and always refused to be charmed. Her life belonged to the children she would teach. She fixed her attention on the floorboards. "What was so important you had to work on a Sunday?"

He balanced the plate on his palm and speared a piece of venison with the fork. "When everyone was in here this morning, I noticed some movement in the floorboards. I didn't want you to trip on a loose board during your first day teaching tomorrow."

"Oh." A wisp of hair escaped her braid and she tucked it in. "That was thoughtful."

"I'm always thinking of you."

"Don't say those things or I will have to leave." She paced to the edge of the empty room with no intention of leaving, and stopped in front of the north-facing window. Outside, pretty Peggy Cotter and her mother, Mrs. Cora Cotter, were ambling through the picnic area, whispering. Peggy's honey-hued hair was arranged in a puffy bun and she wore a corset despite the ban of corsets the group agreed upon before they sailed from America two years ago.

As Peggy and Mrs. Cotter passed the Fosters' picnic blanket, Mrs. Cotter pointed across the road. When Peggy turned to look in that direction, Mrs. Cotter stooped to peek inside the Fosters' food basket. As Peggy turned back to her mother, she spotted Olivia looking at them from inside the chapel. Peggy spoke to Mrs. Cotter, who snapped her gaze toward the chapel. Mrs. Cotter's wiry hair framed her wild-eyed stare.

Olivia pretended not to see them and backed away from the window. Mrs. Cotter's demeanor had changed since the voyage, and her attitude was rubbing off on her four daughters, Peggy included. Olivia walked to the front of the high-ceilinged sanctuary and tried to forget about Peggy and Mrs. Cotter.

Gabe was watching Olivia. She could feel it. She tried to divert his focus. "How long will it take you and your father to build the pews?"

"A couple of weeks. The gray leaf lumber is easy to work with. That's the reason we've been able to build so much so fast."

"What about the school desks?"

"Reverend Colburn said only pews and a lectern in the chapel."

She spun on her heel. "No desks?"

"Sorry, Liv." Gabe shoveled a forkful of potato into his mouth. "Not in the chapel."

"When did Reverend Colburn decide that?"

This time he finished chewing before he spoke. "At the elder meeting last week."

"Why wasn't I informed?"

Gabe shrugged. "What does it matter? The children can sit on the pews."

"Their writing will suffer. We had school desks in Virginia."

"Because we had a schoolhouse in Virginia. Reverend Colburn says he prefers the chapel to be used only for church. He wants to instill respect for it and says if the children use the sanctuary as their playground all week, they won't have reverence on Sundays."

"Then build a separate schoolhouse."

"You can't demand to have something built for the settlement." He handed the empty plate to her. "The elders make all the village decisions."

"You are training to become an elder. Can't you suggest it?"

Gabe shook his head. "That isn't how it works, Liv. Everyone is supposed to take their concerns to their family's elder. Yours is your father. He will decide if it's a matter for the council to hear."

"I thought we left America to start a simpler society."

"Even simple societies need a governing system. So far, one elder per family works for us. Could you imagine what it would be like if we followed through on every idea every person suggested?" He grinned in the way men do when trying to placate a woman with charm.

It was infuriating.

Her cheeks heated and she curled her toes inside her shoes. "I want my students to have desks so they can concentrate and learn."

He tilted his chin. "If it were up to me, I'd build you a schoolhouse with a desk for every child, and for you," he motioned to the front of the chapel, "a long desk with locking drawers and a blackboard from ceiling to chair rail."

"Sounds wonderful." Her feet relaxed. "Suggest that to the elders."

Gabe looked away.

She hadn't meant to be pushy. He usually chuckled at her whenever her assertiveness got the better of her. Not this time. He seemed mature in a way she'd never seen him before—almost solemn. "What is the matter?"

He ran a hand through his thick brown hair but didn't answer. No charming joke, no change of subject, just silence.

She stepped forward. "Gabriel, tell me."

He picked up his hammer and wiped dust from its claw. "We aren't supposed to talk about council meetings, but I know I can trust you." He glanced at the empty doorway. "The elders were divided over the school. Most of the men wanted to keep their children home to help with the chores. Homesteading is harder work than the families foresaw. They need all the help they can get. Why do you think there have been half, a dozen babies born in the past year? Some of the men are afraid we don't have enough people here to make a decent life for the next generation. They think our survival is at stake and it's more important than book learning. They don't see the need for formal education, considering our circumstances—"

"That is absurd! Look at the harvest everyone had this year. Our barns are full and root cellars are packed for the winter."

"No, Liv, it's not absurd."

"Yes, it is." Her volume rose. "The settlement is stable. Children should be in school."

"Shouldn't parents make the decisions about their children's education?"

"Of course..." Olivia took a step back. "Of course they should, so long as they make the right choice... and that is to send children to school."

"That is your opinion."

More strands of hair escaped her experimental braid. She didn't bother trying to tuck them back. "Every child deserves a proper education. I am ready to teach. I haven't spent two years making lesson plans for nothing."

"Some of the elders agree with you. They want their children in school this year and suggested we use the chapel. Since the vote was split, they allowed Jonah to vote because he is a parent now. He voted to start school. He knows how important this is to you... and how important you are to me." Gabe lowered his voice. "This was the most divisive matter the council has dealt with. You would be wise to take what you have been given and forget the rest. Someday we will have a schoolhouse in Good Springs, but not yet. Most of the men are tired of building, and the carpentry work is left to my father and me. We wouldn't mind, but as long as we are building and not farming, the village has to provide for our family."

"We all trade and barter and help each other. That was supposed to be the basis of our society: we all work and we all eat. Can't you at least mention building a schoolhouse to Reverend Colburn?"

Gabe opened his mouth to speak, but glanced behind her and stopped short.

Jonah and Marian Ashton stepped inside the chapel. Marian held their infant son, Frederick, and made the perfect silhouette of a young mother as she stood in the arched doorway, backlit by the autumn sunshine.

Olivia gave Marian a weary smile. They could convey with a glance what could not be said—one thousand memories, their feelings, hopes, and fears, candlelit sleepovers, shared sufferings and triumphs and secrets.

Seeing her best friend hold her firstborn child—the proof of their adult lives—jolted her into the present. This was it... what she had trained and planned and worked for... fulfilling her calling as the first teacher in the new settlement of Good Springs.

Jonah glanced between Olivia and Gabe. He raised an eyebrow. "Are we interrupting something?"

"Kind of," Gabe replied, giving Jonah a look.

"No." Olivia ignored it and moved close to Marian to see the baby. "You aren't interrupting. I brought Gabriel some food. It is the least I could do since he's making sure the chapel is ready for school tomorrow."

CHAPTER TWO

At nine o'clock Monday morning, Olivia stood on the chapel's stone steps, poised and ready with a brass bell in hand. Her insides fluttered as she gave a sidelong glance to Reverend Colburn. He checked his pocket watch and responded with a noble nod.

The autumn wind carried gold and crimson leaves and the scent of wood-burning stoves. Beneath the unending blue sky, eight cabins—one for each of the families that sailed aboard the *Providence*—shadowed the road across from the chapel. Mr. McIntosh and Gabriel McIntosh had expanded some of the cabins into comfortable homes, but a few of the families had gone on to build farmhouses outside the village where they could work the fertile soil. When a family moved out, their old cabin in the village became a workshop. One was now Mr. Roberts' printing press, one for glass making, and one a blacksmith shop.

In the middle of the workshops, a vacant sandy lot marked where the families initially camped under shelters made from the sails of the *Providence*. Olivia believed they should build the schoolhouse on that lot, but her father had ignored her request. He insisted she could teach school in the new chapel just as comfortably.

Schoolhouse or no, this settlement was now her home: a place once unknown, made productive by work, comfortable by family and friends and food, and now inseparable from the hearts that lived therein. She wouldn't leave if she could, especially now that all she'd worked for finally was coming to fruition. She smiled and rang the bell.

Children trekked down the road from both the north and the south ends of the settlement, some escorted by a parent, most flanked by siblings. It felt like back-to-school time in Accomack County, Virginia, and for a moment Olivia forgot Good Springs was a settlement on an uncharted land somewhere in the South Atlantic Ocean.

Mrs. Lillian Colburn was the first to arrive with her children. The reverend's wife wore a cornflower blue shawl draped over her shoulders and held a one-year-old baby on her hip. She pushed a wicker pram with the other hand.

The reverend met his pretty wife at the bottom of the stairs. He kissed her and then pushed his spectacles higher on his nose as he peeked into the pram at his newborn son. Lillian waved a gloved hand, and five of her eight children politely climbed the steps for school.

Olivia paused ringing the bell and greeted the Colburn children as they passed her. "Good morning, Ruth, Virginia, Roseanna. Hello, Anthony. Good morning, Billy."

"Good morning, Miss Owens," each child replied in turn, then stepped into the church and joined Olivia's four youngest siblings.

Lillian raised her elegant brow. "Thank you, Olivia, or Miss Owens, rather. Do send them home promptly at two o'clock, please."

"I will. Where is Johnny?"

The reverend and Lillian exchanged a look, and he returned to the steps. "We will allow you to teach our younger children for the time being, but we will see to their secondary education at home, beginning with Johnny."

"But he hasn't been in school for two years. There is much to review."

Reverend Colburn crossed his long arms. "We have kept up with his instruction at home. Thank you, Miss Owens," he said in a calm but dismissive tone and turned to leave with his wife.

The pounding of hammers across the road broke the quiet of the morning. The far side of Doctor Ashton's house was visible from the top chapel step. Doctor Ashton and two of his sons were working with Mr. McIntosh and Gabe to build an addition onto the Ashton house.

Dust flew on the road as the youngest Ashton boy and his sister raced each other toward the chapel. James won, but Sarah wasn't far behind. They panted their greetings to Olivia as they climbed the stone steps. Once they were inside the church, she continued ringing the bell.

To the north, the three youngest McIntosh children stepped out of their house. Mrs. McIntosh followed them out to the porch. She kissed nine-year-old Barnabus on the top of his head and signed something to him before he left. Deaf since birth, Barnabus might be Olivia's most challenging student. She was familiar with many of the hand motions he used to communicate, but she had planned special lessons for him using pictures and new hand motions. If she could learn to read between bouts of not being able to see words, she could teach him words without using sound. She felt the commonality of their struggles, but he had an advantage in that others knew about his impairment.

Only one person knew Olivia's secret.

The youngest two of the Roberts children were behind the McIntoshes on the road. And as Olivia continued ringing the bell, Peggy Cotter came into view, escorting two of her siblings from their farm north of the settlement. Honey-blond ringlets bounced on either side of Peggy's perfectly voluminous chignon.

Olivia switched the bell to the other hand while waiting for some sign of the Vestal children and Benjamin Foster. Their families' farms were the farthest from the chapel and in opposite directions, but they all should have heard the bell. She wouldn't be surprised if Benjamin had been distracted on the way or decided to play hooky in the grove on the first day of school, but the Vestal children were well behaved. They should have been here by now.

Peggy arrived at the church with Conrad and little Jane. She didn't say goodbye to her siblings but shooed them up the chapel steps. She stayed on the bottom step and craned her neck toward the house where Gabe and the others were working on the Ashtons' addition. She finally looked away from the men, smoothing the top of her puffy bun. "My mother said to tell you to let them come home at noon."

Olivia fingered her plain braid. "The children were supposed to bring their lunch and eat here."

"Mother doesn't want them to go home to eat lunch. She wants them to be finished with school by noon and go home to work."

"The elders agreed school hours are from nine till two. That leaves plenty of daylight for chores."

Peggy shook her head and her iron-formed curls bounced. "Mother said noon. There is a terrible amount of work to be done. The spring box in our creek is too full of milk and it will spoil soon. She needs the girls to help churn butter."

"Butter?" Olivia wanted to inveigh against the Cotters' disregard for the school hours, not to mention her work of preparing lessons and teaching class—all for butter. How disrespectful! Besides, the Owens family's milk cow gave less and less milk each day, and they certainly didn't have enough to make butter.

Olivia would deign to Mrs. Cotter's request to send her children home early, but she wouldn't excuse her for the three children who hadn't been sent to school. "Fine. I will send them home at noon, but only today. Your other siblings are tardy. When will they be here?"

Peggy ignored her and returned her gaze to the men across the road.

"Peggy?" Olivia lifted a palm, wanting an explanation for the absent Cotter children.

"What?" Peggy shrugged. "I thought I heard Gabriel call my name."

He hadn't and wasn't even looking in their direction.

Olivia moved down the steps. "Frances is old enough to decide whether or not she wants to finish school, but where are Judah and Editha and Eveline this morning? All of the children in Good Springs deserve a proper education."

Peggy ignored that too. "By the by, I saw you in the chapel with Gabriel yesterday. I do hope he wasn't tormenting you again."

"Not at all."

"I know how he says sweet things to you, but I always feel so terribly sorry for you when he laughs about it afterward." Peggy fluffed the lace at the end of her sleeves as she spoke. "He says the sweetest things to me too, but he knows I see through his games. He can be such a cad. I do fear someday you'll fall for his jokes."

"Don't worry. I won't." Olivia began to climb back up the steps, but Peggy took hold of her wrist.

"He flirts with the older girls now too, you know. He has my sister Frances intrigued with him and so is Cecelia Foster. I do wish he'd learn to control himself."

Peggy's words felt like a dull blade being thrust between Olivia's ribs, but she couldn't be angry with her. Though Peggy had a bold fondness for herself, she had also kept Olivia well warned of Gabriel's charms. She had hoped he would grow out of his childish amusements by now, but according to Peggy he had not.

Olivia couldn't let it matter. They weren't children anymore, and there were children who needed her. She patted Peggy's hand. "Thank you for bringing the children to school. I will send them home at noon today."

Dimples pitted Peggy's rosy cheeks. "Excellent. And if you are looking for Benjamin Foster, he's around the side of the chapel, hiding behind the lumber pile." Peggy snapped a fake smile at the Vestal children as she walked away.

Olivia climbed to the top of the steps and leaned over the wooden railing to peer around the side of the chapel. Instead of behaving like a disciplined twelve-year-old, Benjamin was crouching by the lumber, holding a magnifying glass over an insect. "Benjamin? Leave that poor creature alone and come inside for class, please."

Benjamin twitched and his hair dropped over his eye as he looked up at her. "I wasn't doing anything wrong," he grumbled.

Two of the Vestal children ascended the steps, and Olivia wanted to make sure they had a pleasant greeting on their first day of school. She quickly leaned back over the railing once more. "Come inside, please, Benjamin."

She turned her attention to young Wade and Doris Vestal. "Good morning, children." She glanced down the road to the north. "Will Hannah and David be joining us this morning?"

Doris stared at her feet.

Wade slurred through crooked front teeth. "Father said David has to work in the orchard. And Hannah has to take care of the babies because Mother couldn't get out of bed today."

Olivia recalled Susanna Vestal's exhaustion at the picnic. "Is your mother all right?"

"She says she's just tired. But sometimes nobody can wake her." Wade scrunched his nose. "And sometimes she wakes up all right and then later she gets tired but doesn't make it back to the bed before she falls over."

"Falls over?" Olivia put a hand on his shoulder. "Has Doctor Ashton been to see her?"

Wade shrugged. "I guess," he said as he looked into the church behind her. Laughter rose as the children who were waiting for class began to play in the big empty room.

Olivia pointed toward the entrance. "Go on inside, children." She gave one last glance in each direction. No one else was coming.

Across the road, Henry Roberts stood in the open doorway of his father's printing shop, keeping a watchful eye on the cauldron full of flax boiling over the fire pit out front. To the south, Gabe and his father were working with the Ashtons on their home addition. The rest of the adults would be on their farms, in their barns or vegetable patches or homes.

She was alone and in charge of her first class. A room of twenty-one children awaited her instruction. This was what she was made for.

Standing near the arched door, she held the bell to her chest and prayed before she went inside. She lifted her face toward the clear blue sky. "Thank you, Lord, for entrusting me with these children. Let my words speak Your wisdom and may Your strength sustain me. And when I look at the page, please let me see the words."

Olivia stepped into the chapel and pulled the heavy wooden door closed behind her. The children stopped talking and turned to look at her. Their expectant stares made her stomach flutter. The calculated steps to the front of the room and the confident speech she had planned dissolved into an awkward shuffle through the scattering of children and a mumble about wishing there were desks.

She lifted her lesson plan book from the floor and willed her spine to straighten as she neared the same spot on the hardwood floor where Reverend Colburn had stood yesterday to deliver his sermon. Though her knees vibrated beneath her skirt, her volition kept her standing. She ran her finger down the roster and smiled, just as her mother always had when she taught. "Good morning, class."

When her greeting was met with silence, a lump formed in her throat, disseminating all hope of establishing her authority. She swallowed hard and glanced at the closed chapel door. Though surrounded by a room full of other human beings, she was alone. "We don't have pews to sit on yet, but we will still sit in rows by age so we can share books. Remember your place on the floor and sit in the same spot each day."

She flipped to her seating chart and pointed at the floor near her feet. "Nearest the front will be our seven-year-old pupils. Billy, Jane, and Doris, please sit here in a row. Behind them, Anthony, Sarah, and Conrad." She stepped away from the front as the children sat where she instructed. "Next, our nine-year-olds: Richie, Virginia, Roseanna, and Barnabus."

The children took their places, except for Barnabus McIntosh, who hadn't heard her instruction. He stood by the window on the south side of the room, watching his big brother work on the home addition across the road. She touched Barnabus' hand and he started. A few of the children giggled as she led him to his seat. If it happened again, she would lecture them on treating others kindly, but she couldn't begin the first day of school with a scolding.

After Barnabus sat on the floor, Olivia checked her roster. "Wade, you will be my only ten-year-old student this year, for now at least. Perhaps the children who stayed home will join us for school once they see how much we all enjoy learning."

One of the older students chortled.

She ignored it and formed the next row. "You may sit with the eleven-year-olds for now, which will be Martha, Edward, Ruth, and Ellenore. Our last row will be our twelve-year-olds: Almeda, Sally, and Ben—" She glanced around the room. "Benjamin didn't come inside, did he?"

Her sister Alice hurried to the door. "I'll tell him to come in."

"Yes, thank you, Alice." As she returned to the front of the room, she motioned to the two adolescents who were standing at the back. "Hazel and James are two of our senior students, as is Alice. Since they have completed their primary education, they will be your monitors. They will be assisting you in your lessons and make sure you stay focused and quiet. Though they are monitors, they are continuing their education and will receive special assignments, as you will once you are their age… if your parents allow it."

Alice returned with Benjamin in tow. Everyone turned to gawk at him, and a mixture of snickers and whispers broke out. Olivia's mother would have reprimanded Benjamin to make an example of his misbehavior, but he looked too pitiful for Olivia to administer harsh treatment. His shaggy hair partially covered his downcast eyes and his freckled nostrils flared. He didn't want to be in school and he certainly didn't want the attention.

"Thank you, Alice. Benjamin, your seat is beside Sally and Almeda."

The anxious children fidgeted and shifted their legs while sitting on the hardwood floor. It was more comfortable than when she helped her mother teach lessons in the stairwell of the ship. That was two years ago and the children were younger with nothing else to entertain them.

Girls began to whisper and boys stared out the windows. Olivia raised her voice to regain their attention. "We have a limited supply of readers, so we will have to share until Mr. Roberts can print more materials." She lifted a stack of books. "One for each learning level. Since everyone here either started school in Virginia or had lessons on the ship, you should be able to keep up with your grade level. But if you have difficulty, simply ask one of the monitors for extra help. Jane, get your finger out of your nose. Do not mark in the books." She continued to distribute the readers but stopped when she reached the fifth graders. "Martha, Ruth, please save your conversation for recess." She tried to get Edward's attention, but his gaze was fixed on something outside the north window. "Edward?"

"Smoke!" he yelled as he jumped to his feet and pointed at the window. "Smoke!"

A thin fog quickly turned into a thick haze. It billowed outside and roiled against the windowpane. Gasps from the older children and timid cries from the young filled the chapel.

Olivia rushed to the window. Tongues of orange flames engulfed the lumber piled beside the chapel. "Everyone outside!" she yelled over the din of cries.

Staying with the children, she shepherded them as they surged to the door. Barnabus broke away from the group and ran back for the schoolbooks scattered at the front of the chapel. As he began snatching the readers from the floor, the smell of smoke wafted into the chapel.

Olivia wanted to save their precious few books as much as he did, but it wasn't worth risking injury or death. "Barnabus!" He couldn't hear her, but she yelled anyway as she dashed to him. "We have to get out!" She yanked on his sleeve and he dropped one of the books. He looked up at her and, though only nine, his steel blue eyes were as piercing as his older brother's. She pulled him to the door and pointed at the house where Gabe was working. "Go get your brother!"

As Barnabus sprinted down the road, Olivia urged the younger children to move away from the building. The older boys ran around the side of the chapel to see the burning lumber, except Benjamin Foster, who hurried across the churchyard toward the grove. She remembered seeing him at the lumber pile with a magnifying glass before class. He had found a way to avoid school after all.

Henry dashed from his father's shop across the road with a bucket, water sloshing over its sides. When he reached the burning gray leaf lumber, he tossed the water into the fire. Steam hissed from one doused flame, but the fire blazed, unabated.

Olivia turned to the older girls. "Alert all the men in the settlement. Tell them to bring water before the burning lumber pile catches the church on fire."

She spotted a shovel propped against the side of one of the workshops. Two of the little girls were hanging onto her skirt, weeping. She pointed across the road and yelled to her young sister, "Almeda! Go and get me that shovel!"

While Almeda ran for the shovel, Olivia knelt to be eye level with the frightened children. As she told them everything would be fine, she lifted her skirt and ripped a layer of fabric from her under petticoat.

Almeda was running back with the shovel. Mrs. Cotter stood by a tree near the road, tucking her wiry hair under her brown bonnet. She was a long way from home for a woman who claimed to be so busy her children couldn't stay in school all day.

Some of the children were running to their houses. They would be out of harm's way for now, but as soon as the fire was out, she wanted them back for school. When Almeda arrived with the shovel, Olivia gave her charge of the little girls.

Olivia covered her mouth and nose with the fabric and tied it at the back of her head. Gripping the shovel with both hands, and rushed to the woodpile. "Move away!" she told the boys, who were standing too close to the blaze.

She sank the shovel into the sandy soil, expecting to fill the blade with a scoop of dirt, but the dry ground was hard and cold. She tossed a paltry amount of dirt into the blaze and thrust the shovel into the earth with the ball of her foot again and again, ignoring the strain in her shoulders and back. Her heavy breath moistened the cloth over her mouth.

The wooden boards on the side of the chapel were beginning to blacken from the smoke. Olivia refused to allow Benjamin's blunder with a magnifying glass to burn down the chapel. It had taken the men months to build it. Her books were inside and years of handwritten lesson plans and hand drawn figures for when her written words lost their meaning. The smoke stung her eyes, but she kept throwing dirt onto the fire.

Her arms began to weaken, but she plunged the shovel blade into the dirt. It hit a rock and vibrated the length of her arms with a dull and deep ache. At once, the shovel was pulled from her hands.

"Get back!" Gabe commanded as he thrust the shovel into the soil. He gave her a quick glance. She expected him to scowl or look shocked, but he wore a partial grin.

Henry arrived with another bucket of water, and between their efforts, the fire was out within seconds.

She untied the cloth from her face and blinked until she produced enough tears to sooth the dry burn stinging her eyes. When she turned her back to the ruined lumber pile and surveyed the lawn from the church to the road, only half her students were in sight. The rest of the frightened children had scattered to their homes.

Mothers were beginning to appear on porches, wiping their hands on their aprons, trying to figure out what the commotion was. Fathers were coming with buckets, but it was too late. The lumber for the church pews was ruined, but the chapel was saved. The blackened window and siding could be scrubbed and sanded to look like nothing had happened.

As Olivia tried to call for the children to return, her throat stung. She needed a moment to catch her breath and will herself not to cry. Reverend Colburn walked toward the chapel with two of the Colburn children on the road behind him. They had alerted their father. Good, maybe he would help her get the children back inside for class.

Olivia trudged to the chapel steps. The Reverend held up a finger as he passed her and hurried to the flame-marked side of the chapel. She wiped her face, combed her hair back into place with her fingers, and brushed the dirt from her hem while she waited for him to return.

After a moment of muffled men's voices, Henry and the others, holding empty buckets, left the churchyard. Gabe walked around the corner with the shovel in one hand. He looked at Olivia, but he wasn't grinning any longer. He squeezed her shoulder as he passed her.

Finally, the reverend returned to the front of the church building. He raised his voice for the crowd. "Everyone, go back to your homes and your work today. School is hereby canceled. The elders are to meet here at sundown. Please, spread the word. Good day to you all." He whirled past Olivia and up the steps. "Miss Owens, come with me."

As she followed the reverend into the chapel, he blew out a frustrated breath. Even during the arduous voyage when they sailed from America to this unpopulated land, she had never witnessed him showing impatience. The schoolbooks were scattered about the room. She wanted to pick them up but didn't.

The reverend paced to the blackened window and shook his head. "I never should have allowed this misuse of God's house."

"Reverend Colburn, I know the children were frightened by the fire, but they are all safe and everything is all right."

"The lumber for the church's furniture is ruined."

"Yes, I understand. But the students and the chapel are fine." She bent to pick up one of the readers. The embossed letters on the book's spine were inscrutable marks, but by its burgundy cover, she recognized the third grade reader. "Perhaps after an hour or so the chapel will air out, and I can bring the students back to class."

"No. Collect your things and return home."

His command gripped her insides like an iron vise clamp. Her jaw hardened as she struggled to find her voice. "I—I believe it would ease their minds to come back inside and see that everything is indeed fine."

"Indeed not. Tell your father the elders will meet here at sundown."

"But, sir—"

"Good day, Miss Owens."

CHAPTER THREE

Olivia sat on the stoop of Marian's cabin, waiting alone. The oval moon's bluish light spilled over her skin and the porch and the cleared land between Marian and Jonah's home and the chapel where the elders were meeting to discuss the fire damage. Oil lanterns filled the distant chapel windows with warm light, but it wasn't enough for Olivia to see what was happening inside the church. Hopefully, the elders were deciding to allow school to resume tomorrow.

Shadows from the nearby gray leaf trees streaked the lawn around the moonlit house while Marian was inside tucking the baby into his cradle. Peace emanated from Marian and Jonah's cozy home. If only it could calm Olivia's anxious heart tonight.

A cold breeze brought a chill through her woolen shawl. When she shivered, her aching shoulder muscles burned. She untied the ribbon from her braid and combed out the long strands with her fingers. Her thick hair covered her neck and back. The scent of smoke clung to every tress. It probably looked as terrible as it smelled, but after such a wearisome day, vanity lost to fatigue.

Marian tiptoed out of the cabin and pulled the door closed, save a two-inch gap. She put her ear to it for a moment. Olivia held her breath, also trying to listen for the baby.

Complete silence.

Marian left the door cracked. "He is asleep," she said softly as she sat beside Olivia on the porch steps.

"I'm sorry to bother you at night," Olivia whispered.

"You don't have to whisper. Frederick will sleep until his next feeding. And you are never a bother to me."

"I thought the elders would be done with their meeting by now."

Marian planted her palms behind her on the porch and lifted her face to the starry sky. "When the elders meet at sundown, I don't expect Jonah home for hours."

Olivia looked up too, but the stars could not hold her attention. Her eyes returned to the chapel and the one blackened window. The marred glass mocked her attempt at establishing a school for the remote settlement. The first day after a crisis was always the hardest and she probably wasn't the most anxious person tonight. She glanced at Marian. "Did you see Benjamin or your parents after the fire?"

"Father stopped here to see the baby on his way to the meeting tonight. He said Ben wouldn't answer him when he asked why he started the fire."

"Did Benjamin admit he was responsible?"

"No. Father said he wouldn't speak."

"Does your father think he did it?"

"Of course. Several of the children saw Ben by the lumber with his magnifying glass. Mother said he was probably trying to burn bugs as usual and he accidentally caught the wood on fire."

"So it *was* an accident then."

"It's hard to know when Ben is involved. He simply won't respond to questioning anymore." Marian pulled her gaze away from the sky and brushed her palms together. "Maybe my brother doesn't belong in school. He's content in the pasture, tending the sheep and helping Father, but as soon as he comes into the village, he ends up being accused of something. My family would understand if you didn't allow him to go back to class."

Olivia hadn't considered banning the young man from school. There would always be a troublemaker. Her mother used to say those children needed more challenging assignments. But if Benjamin Foster did not want to be in school, it wasn't worth having him burn the building down. She shrugged one shoulder. "I will leave it up to him and your parents. What did Jonah say when he heard about the fire?"

Marian tucked a wisp of blond hair behind her ear. "He was grateful no one was hurt, especially you, after the way you went at the fire with a shovel. He wasn't surprised Ben was blamed, if that's what you mean."

It wasn't what she meant. "Was Jonah disappointed?"

"In Ben?"

"No... that school was canceled for the day... that Reverend Colburn canceled school."

"Ah—" Marian gave an understanding nod. "Are you seeking allies?"

"No, not at all."

"I will always take your side. I don't care what the issue might be."

"Thank you, but I would never try to get anyone to take my side against the reverend. I don't want there to be sides." She tucked her skirt around her legs from her knees to her ankles. "I'm not against Reverend Colburn. Jonah has the best education of everyone here our age, and so I wondered what he thought about this canceling school on a whim."

"Well, it wasn't on a whim. Reverend Colburn was concerned for the children and for the chapel." Marian put a hand to Olivia's back. It was the first comforting touch she had felt all day. "Jonah admires how you have championed education for the settlement now that your mother is no longer able to teach."

Her mother was able to teach; she simply didn't want to anymore. A lack of desire and a lack of ability were two different things. No matter. Olivia possessed both the desire and ability. It was the support of her peers she questioned. She rubbed her cold fingers together. "What about the others? What do they think?"

"They who?"

"Those of us who aren't children, but don't have school-age children yet."

Marian lifted a palm. "What does it matter?"

"It matters to me." She shivered and blew warm air into her cupped hands. "The parents have openly expressed their opinions on sending their children to school. And the children seem to have mixed feelings about it. My mother says that will never change. But what about our group... you and Jonah... and Henry and Peggy and Gabriel?"

"You know Jonah and I support you and will be grateful to have a school established here for our children when the time comes." Marian furrowed her brow as she thought for a moment. "I haven't spoken to Henry since the picnic, but he only talks about the printing press and their progress with making paper. And who cares what Peggy thinks?"

"I do. Sometimes."

Peggy's opinions had the power to encourage and shatter in equal measure. At the moment, Olivia did not need any more shattering. She waved a hand as if swatting away the thought of Peggy Cotter. "What about Gabriel?"

Marian grinned. "I think you already know what Gabe thinks of you."

"Not of me... of the school."

"I don't know if I've ever heard him say."

Olivia tightened her shawl around her shoulders. "I thought maybe Jonah tells you what the men talk about in the elder meetings."

"All I know is that Gabe is finishing the building projects for the other families." Marian faced the chapel and the moonlight highlighted her delicate features. "And then the men are going to help him clear land to build his own house."

"His own house? I hadn't heard."

"The elders decided last week. Each family's elder is supposed to pass on settlement news to the family."

"My father doesn't tell us anything. Not me anyway. He probably tells Walter everything." She glanced across the road and to the north toward her family's house. The McIntoshes house was the next property to the north. Neither home was visible from here at night through the trees. She buried her hands beneath her shawl. "Where is Gabe going to build his house?"

"Beside Mr. Weathermon's cabin near the big stream. Jonah goes to check on Mr. Weathermon every day, and sometimes Gabe goes along. He likes that area." Marian stood and pointed at the chapel. "The meeting must be over. I can see figures moving in the chapel."

Olivia stood too and wiped her palms on her skirt. "Let's hope they made the right decision."

Moments later, the crackling of footsteps on twigs came from the road as Jonah walked toward the cabin.

Olivia glanced at Marian. "I guess I should go home and wait for my father."

"He is still at the chapel," Jonah said as he approached.

Gabe was with him. He looked at her with his expression stoic. An unwelcomed clench tightened inside Olivia's chest. She had not started the fire that destroyed his lumber, but she suddenly felt the grip of guilt. "Gabe, I want you to know how sorry I am the wood for the church pews was ruined. I know the fire gave you more work to do and you have already done so much for the settlement."

Gabe raised a hand to halt her apology, but she continued so he wouldn't have a chance to tell her he was disappointed about the fire or in Benjamin or in her. "I didn't know you were trying to finish all the carpentry work in the village so you could start building your own house."

"Liv—"

"Not that if I had known I could have done anything else to extinguish the fire. I tried. Really, I did."

Jonah slid his arm around Marian's waist. "We should go inside. Goodnight, Olivia. Goodnight, Gabriel."

"Goodnight," they replied in unison as their closest friends quietly slipped into the cabin.

Olivia watched the door. Even after it closed she stared, hoping Marian would come back outside. She had Marian's support. If Gabe was angry with her or had taken Reverend Colburn's side—even though she didn't want there to be sides—at least she had Marian.

"Liv?"

"Pardon?"

Gabe pointed a thumb toward the road. "I asked if I could walk you home."

"Yes, of course."

She scanned the woods to the north of Marian and Jonah's cabin. The moonlight did little to brighten the forest beyond the first few trunks of gray leaf trees. Never before had she felt frightened at night in this land. Nothing in the forest had changed. The same nocturnal animals that foraged through the underbrush last night were here tonight. The same birds roosted in the limbs above the road. The same misshapen moon lent its glow to the silvery foliage of the gray leaf trees.

The cold had silenced the crickets and she missed their song. The quiet and the chill and the darkness stirred discontent deep in her spirit. And knowing people were speaking about her in a less than pleasant manner added bile to the ill feeling.

Gabe reached for her hand and gently tucked it around his arm as they started walking to the road. "It cooled down quickly this evening."

Her patience was too drained to talk about the weather. "What did the elders decide? Can I teach school tomorrow?"

He smoothed her fingers over his arm, the palms of his callused hands warm and wide. "Your father stayed after the meeting to speak with Reverend Colburn privately."

"So Jonah said." Olivia glanced at Gabe as they left Marian and Jonah's property and walked onto the sandy road. "But they made a decision before you left the meeting, right?"

Twigs snapped in the brush near the road. The muscles in Gabe's arm tightened beneath her hand. He gave the woods a quick glance. His breath forced steady white puffs into the cold air. "Probably a deer."

His face was striking in the moonlight—eyes narrowed with focus, jaw set with confidence. She forced herself to look away while she waited for him to answer her questions, but he said nothing.

The smoking chimney of her family's home came into view. Gabe had never escorted her on his arm like this before. She would think it a sweet gesture if his lack of grins and jokes didn't betray his angst. Normally, she appreciated a man's solemn politeness, but knowing Gabe, it was disconcerting.

She asked, "Are you angry with me about the ruined lumber?"

"No." He slowed their pace. "Why would you think that?"

"Because I apologized to you, and you didn't say you forgave me."

He kept his voice soft. "I didn't need to forgive you because you did me no wrong. The fire wasn't your fault. No matter what they say, it wasn't your fault."

"They? What do you mean?"

She started to pull her hand off his arm, but he held it there as they strode toward her family's home.

She watched him and he watched the road. "You aren't answering me."

"Not for my sake."

"What did the reverend decide about school? That was the purpose of the meeting, wasn't it?"

"You have to ask your elder. That's the rule and since I'm going to become an elder someday, I have to follow the rules." He turned toward her family's house and walked her to the porch. "I want to give you everything you dream of, Liv."

Peggy always said Gabe told her things like that too. Olivia had almost believed him once and had sworn to herself she never would again. Only now his words were not accompanied by smiles and winks. When he was trying to charm her, it was easier to believe he was the insincere flirt Peggy claimed he was. But now the straight line of his lips and the slight rise of his brow marked his expression with concern.

She let go of his arm. "Tell me you will be on my side."

He spread his palms. "There isn't much I can do."

"Even if you can't do anything, I want to know I have your loyalty... in friendship."

"Of course." He leaned a degree closer. "Of course, my loyalty... and friendship and so much more... if only you would let me."

She took a step back and disappointment flashed across his face. She couldn't let it matter. She wouldn't let him charm her. Still, regret lurked beneath the surface of her guarded heart like a corpse beneath an icy pond.

Gabe lowered his chin, and in the moonlight, his blue eyes looked black. "Goodnight, Liv."

"Goodnight," she whispered.

As Gabe walked back to the road, he passed her father. The men exchanged a lighthearted word that drew a chuckle from Mr. Richard Owens. As Gabe disappeared toward his family's home, Richard neared the house. He aimed a work-worn finger at the door. "Go inside, Livy."

She turned to the porch, obediently. The fire in the hearth illumined the glass in the window. Her mother and Alice were sitting in the parlor, knitting, with Almeda and Martha nearby. She might be forbidden to attend the elder meetings, but whatever their verdict, she did not want it delivered in front of her young sisters. She faced her father. "What did Reverend Colburn decide?"

Richard crossed his arms over his chest. "Gabriel didn't tell you?"

"No. He said I was to ask my family's elder."

"Good man. He will make a fine elder someday." Richard rubbed his swollen knuckles together. Thirty years of cutting and laying stone had disfigured his hands, but he never complained. "Benjamin will not be allowed to ride his horse for a week."

"His horse? Is that why the reverend called a meeting? To figure out how to punish Benjamin?"

Her father shook his head. "No, Mr. Foster informed us of the punishment."

"The way everyone treats Benjamin is punishment enough. The more people distrust him, the harder it is for him to behave respectably. He made a mistake, but I doubt he meant to set the lumber ablaze. The fire was put out and no one was hurt. The elders shouldn't blame him."

"They don't. They blame you."

"What?" Olivia's heart pounded in her throat. "How am I to blame for the fire?"

Richard picked at the thick skin on the heel of his hand. "The elders decided not to allow the chapel to be used for school."

"Are they going to build a schoolhouse?"

"This is no time for you to ask for more, young lady." He glanced at the window behind her. "If you insist on teaching the children, they have agreed to allow you to go house to house for lessons. You may teach at each house one day per week."

One day per week times eight families with school-aged children. She would have to go to two houses per day. That meant each child would have only half a day of school each week. "There is no way I can instill a proper education and love for learning in children who are given one class per week."

Richard shrugged. "If you want to teach, this is your only option."

"One day of school per week for each family will not make education a priority and the elders will never authorize a schoolhouse."

"Take it or leave it. You can have the rest of the week to sort out your schedule with the families and get your lessons ready, then start Monday."

"But, Father—"

"But nothing! Your mother and I have done everything we could for you. If she hadn't been the teacher in Accomack for twenty years, you never would have had the chance to teach here. Most families in the settlement want to keep their children home and I understand. Building a town out of nothing is hard work. You can't blame the elders for this." He wagged a crooked finger at her. "You should be grateful Doctor Ashton spoke up for you at the meeting tonight and I stayed afterward to make sure Reverend Colburn doesn't think any less of our family." He stomped past her to the porch then turned back. "Decide tonight if you want to teach from house to house. If not, I don't want to hear any more about school. We will leave education up to the parents like we should have in the first place."

* * *

Olivia turned over again, unable to find a comfortable position on her half of the feather bed she shared with Alice. She reached to the wooden trunk next to the bedstead and opened her ceramic keepsake box. Her fingers found the silver watch pin—a gift from her late grandmother—nestled in an embroidered handkerchief inside. Her grandmother's lavender scent still clung to the old kerchief. The aroma triggered memories of long winter afternoons sitting on the floor by the rocking chair while her grandmother read stories to her.

Though the moon sent generous light through the windowpane, she couldn't read the time. Perhaps no one had informed the monster that the Roman numerals on four points of the watch face represented numbers, therefore, it should not hide them from her.

It wouldn't matter. There was no monster, just as Doctor Ashton told her when she was little. It wasn't a monster. It wasn't her eyesight. It was just her, but if she wanted to spend her life teaching school, she'd better hope the elders never found out she often lost her ability to read. God hadn't taken the problem away no matter how fervently and humbly she'd beseeched Him. It was her affliction to bear, and she had to bear it silently if she wanted to be a schoolteacher.

None of that seemed to matter now. She'd lost the elders' respect before she'd had the chance to earn it. She had worked to learn and learned to teach and now she had no school to teach in and probably never would.

Though she couldn't read the hour, it felt late. Her three younger sisters were asleep, and the nasally snores leaking through the partition from the other side of the upstairs bedroom assured her that her two brothers were asleep also.

She carefully placed the watch pin back in its soft bedding in her keepsake box atop the trunk between the bed and the corner. Her corner. Each of the six Owens children had claimed a private area of the upstairs room of their family's home. And the corner from the north-facing window ledge to the wall was her space.

She kept a stack of books on the trunk next to the keepsake box and her lantern. Her Bible topped the stack. She tried to keep the other books in the order she'd first read them, but inevitably her favorites rose to the top: *The Pious Minstrel and Christian's Companion: a Collection of Sacred Poetry*, a clothbound copy of *Shakespeare's Sonnets*, and a first edition of *The Scarlet Letter*.

She trailed a finger along the spine of the books. Reading Hawthorne's romantic tale would be a welcome escape from her racing thoughts right now, but she wouldn't be able to see the words if she tried.

Nor could she sleep. Not with half the village blaming her for the fire outside the chapel and the other half already convinced her school was a waste of time.

And below the embarrassment and frustration, Gabriel McIntosh's tender words replayed over and over in her mind. He had promised her *loyalty and friendship and so much more if only…*

She lowered her feet to the floor and straightened her nightgown as she looked through the window to the world outside. A swath of moonlit gray leaf trees blocked her view of the McIntoshes' house next door. Gabe probably was asleep in there. What had he truly meant by *so much more if only you would let me*? Was he the incorrigible flirt Peggy insisted he was or had he sincerely offered his heart?

Olivia's toes curled against the cold floor as she padded down to the parlor. It was not an actual parlor, but an open space between the kitchen and her parent's bedroom. Since her mother called it the *parlor*, the rest of the family had no choice but to follow suit. It was treated more reverently than other areas of the house because it was where Mrs. Mary Owens kept her one treasure from their home in Accomack County, Virginia—an oak rocking chair with a caned back and embroidered cushion.

Though long after midnight, Mary was still sitting in her rocking chair, gazing at the quartered gray leaf log on the grate. A steady golden flame rose from the slowly-consumed wood.

Her mother gave her an appraising glance. "You all right?"

Olivia nodded. It wasn't true. She stood on the rag rug by Mary's chair, hoping her mother would ask her again, but she didn't. "I couldn't sleep."

"Nor I."

Olivia knelt on the rug. "You're disappointed in me, aren't you?"

Her mother didn't immediately answer, and her silence stung more than any word. The wood rockers brushed over the rug rhythmically with every swing of the chair.

Forward... back... forward...

Olivia's tense shoulders rose to her ears. Her fingers burned to grab the oak rocker and halt its movement.

"No, I'm not disappointed in you. At first I was, simply because your father was, but then I realized he is just embarrassed. Now I am disappointed in myself. This was my fault. You helped me in the classroom in Virginia as a monitor when you were a senior student, and you taught some of the lessons on the ship, but that was two years ago. You have never held charge of twenty children in a classroom by yourself. It was my failing not to supervise until you were more experienced."

Olivia's shoulders relaxed. "But if you had been there today Reverend Colburn would have been cocksure you were to blame for the fire and would have canceled your school and made everyone angry with you."

Mary pointed her finger at Olivia but kept her gaze on the fire. "Don't speak of the reverend with that tone. He left the chapel in the care of an inexperienced young woman, against his better judgment—"

Olivia mumbled, "Then perhaps he is to blame."

"And he did not make anyone angry with you. The elders are constantly aware of how vulnerable our settlement is. We are isolated from the world. Everyone has worked their fingers to the bone to build what little we have, and it could all be easily destroyed. If people get hurt here, there isn't any real medicine left. Lives could be lost easily. The fire today reinforced the elders' fear."

"Fear?" She picked at a loop in the rug. "What happened to trusting God with our lives? When we sailed away from America and the *Providence* drifted for over three months, everyone constantly reminded each other to trust God. We did and He brought us here. Have we lost faith now?"

The rocker stopped in the middle of a backward movement. Mary's heels hovered over the floor. She looked at Olivia, wide-eyed. "No, but it seems the elders might have forgotten what God did in the past. Perhaps after the hard work of building a self-sustaining village, they have forgotten who truly provides our sustenance." Her mother gave her a thin smile. "Out of the mouths of babes."

"I'm no babe, Mother."

"You are to me."

"And to the elders?"

"Perhaps."

Olivia poked her little finger through the loop in the rug. "Now what do I do? They said the only way I can teach is if I go from house to house each week. If I do that, the children will not learn as well as they could with daily instruction. Nor would education be made a priority, especially if the elders are afraid for their survival."

Mary resumed rocking. "You're right."

"Father won't help my cause, will he?"

Her mother shook her head. "Not while the current attitude prevails."

"What can we do?

"Pray for them. Pray God changes their hearts. That He proves His loving provision to them once again."

"But it is all around us."

"Then pray the elders see it, with their eyes and in their souls."

Olivia pulled her finger out of the loop. "Until then, what should I do about teaching? I have to give my answer tomorrow."

Mary stretched her arms along the length of the rocking chair's arms and curled her hands around the ornately carved ends. "Do you believe God has called you to teach?"

"Yes."

"And that He has given you the desire, ability, and strength to teach?"

"Yes."

"Then teach however you can, wherever you can, and leave the rest to the Lord."

CHAPTER FOUR

The strap of Olivia's book-filled satchel dug into her shoulder by the time she reached her first teaching appointment. She adjusted the strap as she surveyed the Cotters' enclosed porch. Three splintered trunks were stacked one atop the other, a wad of mildew-freckled burlap fluttered in the breeze, a stove cord of firewood was draped in scraps of threadbare fabric that had been left there to dry and long since hardened.

Perhaps in their desire to live by the adage *waste not want not*, the Cotter family had forgotten *cleanliness is next to godliness*.

This was not how Olivia envisioned teaching school, but it was her only option. The children of this isolated settlement deserved a schoolhouse and daily classes. It was up to her to find a way to make that happen. Until then, she would submit to the elders' decision.

She raised a knuckle and knocked on the Cotters' front door.

"Come in," a child's voice sang from inside.

Olivia reached for the doorknob.

"No! Wait out there," Mrs. Cora Cotter tersely corrected.

Material hanging inside the door's window blocked Olivia's attempt to see what was happening. The pinstripes of the faded calico curtain moved. She expected someone to let her in, but it was the contrasting pattern that tricked her into seeing nonexistent motion.

Dizziness often invited the monster. If it came during the children's reading lesson, she would improvise. With only two young students at the Cotters', she could switch from reading to mathematics or tell them it was time to practice their writing.

She closed her eyes and focused on the sounds around her. Sometimes that made the feeling go away. Footsteps scuffed on the other side of the door. A dog barked behind the house. Waves crashed far in the distance, or it was her imagination; it had been so long since she'd gone to the shore to relax.

The door jerked open, and little Jane wrapped her arms around Olivia's waist. "Thank you for coming to teach me!"

"Oh, it is my pleasure," Olivia wheezed as she loosened Jane's enthusiastic grip on her ribs. She stepped into the cramped house.

Conrad carried an empty crate out the back door, following three of his older sisters who held wooden buckets. Peggy wasn't inside—at least not on the lower level. Olivia listened for movement upstairs but heard nothing.

Mrs. Cotter stood at the stove with her back to the room, scrubbing the range vigorously. A frizzy curl had escaped her bun and rose four inches in the air like a rusted spring. It bounced as she spoke. "Teach Jane first. Conrad has chores to do." She flicked a dour glance over her shoulder at Olivia. "Jane can't subtract to save her soul, so you might want to start with arithmetic." Then she mumbled as she scrubbed, "Not that she will use book learning here ever. None of these children will. We are stuck on this godforsaken island. Stuck forever. We will die here and our children will die here and their children, if they live long enough to have any. Probably starve long before that. We all will."

Olivia's mouth gaped. This land was plentiful—full of game and fertile soil. She studied Mrs. Cotter's figure from behind. The woman had gained a few pounds since moving into the farmhouse even though the physical labor of homesteading kept most of the settlers lean. Maybe she was with child. At forty-two, Mrs. Cotter was the oldest of the women in Good Springs. Pregnancy wasn't impossible, but it didn't seem likely. And everyone would have known by now. Secrets were hard to keep in a settlement this small. Whatever the cause of her weight gain, her bitter remarks were not from a lack of food. No one in this house was starving.

Jane took Olivia by the hand and pulled her to the kitchen table. Long enough to seat the family of nine, the table took up most of the kitchen and part of the sitting area. Its rudimentary construction differed from the fine furniture Gabe built, but it appeared stable.

Olivia set her satchel on the table's edge farthest from the kitchen and withdrew several schoolbooks. She looked at her eager pupil. "Let's start with arithmetic, shall we, Miss Jane?"

"Oh, yes." Jane curled her legs onto the chair. "Did you bring a book for me?"

"I did."

Mrs. Cotter plunked her scrub brush onto a shelf and carried a pail of dirty water out the back. She closed the door, then pinned Olivia with a cold stare through the window for one unnerving moment.

Olivia held her breath until the woman walked away.

An hour passed before Peggy came downstairs and an hour more before Conrad returned to begin his lessons.

Peggy boiled a kettle of water and made herself tea, then sat at the other end of the table. She lifted the steaming cup close to her lips but didn't sip. Though late morning Peggy still looked half asleep.

Little Jane absorbed every moment of her lessons, while Conrad fidgeted and complained. It was nearly noon when Mrs. Cotter returned to the back door. Her other daughters were with her, all sly whispers and deadly glances. Frances was seventeen and had adopted the worst of Mrs. Cotter's negative attributes. The other two girls—ten-year-old twins Editha and Eveline—seemed too young to carry such a quiver full of poisonous stares.

They also carried wooden buckets shrouded with a blackberry stained cloth. Their arms strained as if the covered buckets were full.

Peggy sat with a fabric-covered pillow on her lap, pinning a pattern to make lace. She ignored her sisters as they set the table for lunch, and she ignored her father and brother when they came in to wash up. She glanced at her mother once when Mrs. Cotter mumbled nonsensically as she sliced a loaf of bread.

Olivia slowly gathered her books from the table and arranged her pencils and chalk in her satchel. She half expected to be asked to stay for lunch—perhaps as a display of gratitude for teaching the children. When no one acknowledged her preparations to leave, she carried Jane's slate to Mrs. Cotter. "Jane learns quickly. I made a short list of lessons for her to complete this week, and I will leave one reader for the children to share. It's very important they take good care of the book."

Mrs. Cotter sighed and glared at the book as if its existence taxed her energy. She grabbed the reader and tossed it on the shelf beside the blackened scrub brush. "Waste of time."

As Mrs. Cotter returned her attention to the bread, Jane peeked under the cloth that covered the buckets her sisters had brought inside. The little girl exclaimed, "Three buckets full of blackberries! Oh, I do love blackberries!"

"Shush!" Mrs. Cotter yanked Jane by the hair, pulling her away from the blackberries. "What have I told you about blabbering about our food." Her squinted eyes darted to Olivia. "These are our berries, fair and square." She inched closer and hissed. "Keep your mouth shut about us when you go around the village teaching your little school lessons. Don't be a busybody. God judges busybodies."

Olivia suddenly felt as young and frightened as Jane, but she managed a stiff nod.

Mrs. Cotter jerked her chin toward the front door. "You best get going. I have a family to feed. Good day, Miss Owens."

"Good day." Olivia glanced down at Jane who frowned at the floor. "Goodbye, Jane. I will be back next Monday."

As Olivia slinked away from the kitchen, she eyed the rest of the Cotter family. No one flinched at Mrs. Cotter's rude behavior. Mr. Teddy Cotter washed his hands in the basin by the back door, and his son waited for a turn with the water. The elder daughters argued amongst themselves while they prepared lunch.

Peggy stabbed a pin into the top of the cushion and stood from her lacemaking perch. She met Olivia at the front door and smiled politely. "Don't mind Mother," she whispered as she opened the door for Olivia. "She's just frightfully busy."

As Olivia crossed the threshold, she paused to ask Peggy what had made Mrs. Cotter so bitter, but Peggy shook her head quickly and looked away.

The door closed behind Olivia, and the lock clicked before her feet reached the porch steps. She glanced back and prayed Jane wouldn't be mistreated again. She would speak to Peggy about her mother's behavior the next time they were alone. If that made her a busybody, so be it. Something wasn't right about Mrs. Cotter since coming to this land, and Jane was suffering for it.

As Olivia walked to the road, she pulled a wrapped biscuit from her satchel. Between it and a ripe plum, she had a sufficient midday meal. Staying at the Cotters' house for lunch had never been mentioned, so she alone could be blamed for supposing an invitation would be extended.

Come to think of it, when she had scheduled the children's lessons with Mr. Cotter, he'd acted as though he did her a great favor by allowing her to come to their home. And in a way he had. It was a privilege to teach someone else's children and to set up a school for a morning in their home, yet not so great a privilege that inhospitality should be excused.

Olivia unfurled the cloth from the biscuit as she left the Cotters' farm and stepped onto the road. Pinching off a corner of the crumbly bread, she turned north and ambled toward the Vestals' property.

The chill of the morning air lingered in the forest shadows, so she hurried through the darker places where the trees met high above the road. Once in the sunlight, her dark woolen shawl absorbed the sun's heat. The light ignited silvery specks on the gray leaf foliage all around. Oaks and maples waved leaves flaming with oranges and deep reds, and the mulberry trees glowed with glossy yellow. The green in the forest was left to the pine and the grassy undergrowth.

Heady scents of gray leaf and juniper swirled through the autumn breeze. When she finally came to the meadow before the Vestals' property, the intoxicating aroma, warm sunshine, and blissful quiet of creation lulled her into the peace she craved. She surveyed the area for a place to sit and found a felled tree trunk along the road near the Vestals' orchard.

She sat on the low log and tucked her skirt close to her legs. As she finished her lunch, she counted the rows of two-year-old trees a stone's throw from her. The orchard's rows stretched far into the distance. Twine tied to stakes anchored each sapling, and a blanket of straw encircled their bases. The ground between rows had been recently scythe mowed, keeping the orchard clear and ensuring the Vestals would have fodder for the livestock through the coming winter.

As she drew the plum out of her satchel, Mr. Christopher Vestal rounded a distant row of trees with a wheelbarrow. He stepped onto the sandy road where it dwindled to a path. "Hello, Miss Owens," he called casually and tipped his straw hat.

"Good afternoon, Mr. Vestal." Olivia stood and held up her plum. "I was eating my lunch."

He lowered the wheelbarrow to the ground and brushed dirt from the smock he wore over his work coat. "You're welcome to eat in our kitchen."

"I thought it best to give you and your family time to eat before I went to the house." Not to mention the last family she had called on wanted her out of their way, and she wasn't in a hurry to be found a nuisance again.

"I don't go inside at noon, and the others would have finished eating by now. But Susanna and the children will be happy to have your company. Wade and Doris are especially excited about your visit."

Grateful for the hospitable welcome, she smiled. "Thank you." She pointed at the wide meadow across the road. "I was enjoying this beautiful view."

He picked bits of hay grass from his sleeves and walked toward her. A yellow retriever followed him. When he drew near, he gazed out across the meadow then at his young orchard. "The Lord has given us a fine allotment. This land is far greater than anything I could have asked Him to provide."

The dog greeted Olivia, and she offered it an open hand. "How long before the apple trees begin producing fruit?"

"Six to eight more years." He grinned and golden flecks shone in his brown irises. "Tired of plums and figs, are we?"

"No, no. I simply wondered how you and your family are sustaining yourselves with all of your effort going into the orchard, since it won't produce food for several years."

"Not all of our efforts go into the orchard. We tend a vegetable patch, catch fish in the stream, and harvested a half-acre of wheat, corn, and potatoes this year. And of course, we have a milk cow, though she hasn't given much milk these past few weeks."

"Neither has ours. Only at the evening milking."

"Ours too. She's completely dry in the mornings." A faint furrow marked his brow. "Odd."

"Do you think?"

Mr. Vestal glanced at the road toward the village. "Maybe it's nothing." After a quiet moment, he shrugged then waved his hand for her to walk with him to the house. "Other than the unreliable cow, we have plenty to eat. Our root cellar is full for winter. We are truly blessed—all of us—to be in this land."

She gave the dog a final pat and followed Mr. Vestal to the back of the narrow two-story farmhouse. "You must work from dawn till dusk."

"And my wife and children too." Creases in the skin from the outer corner of his eyes to his temples attested to his age. Wrinkles bespoke maturity on a handsome man but did little to improve the credentials of a middle-aged woman. He lifted his chin to the saplings. "And we must keep working if we want to see the fruit of this orchard. Not just for our family, but for the whole settlement. That is why I cannot allow David to stop for school lessons during the day. He must learn all that I can teach him in the fields. He will have to continue my work should something happen to me."

"I never thought of that," she said as she walked beside him.

"It's the same for all of the men in Good Springs. We have an opportunity to build a fine village, but everyone must do his part, including our children, if we expect the settlement to thrive."

"I don't want to put your family or any of the families to hardship by insisting their children attend school. I believe the children will benefit and help the settlement flourish if they can read and write and understand arithmetic."

Christopher Vestal nodded. "Reading and writing, yes. It is important that they know how to document, how to read, how to study the scripture, but this will be a bartering society with minimal government and, it appears, no contact with other nations. Right now, life skills are of greatest importance."

Olivia raised a finger. "True, but they will need a good understanding of commerce to know if their bartering is fair. If a woman spends a month sewing a quilt, should she trade it for one bushel of your apples?"

He chuckled at her. "You make a convincing argument."

"It is my desire to pass along my knowledge to the next generation as much as it is yours."

"Then I shall allow you that much, Miss Owens." He slowed their pace as they approached the back door of his farmhouse. "For the past two years, I have taught my sons as we went about our days in the fields, and Susanna has taught the girls. We all read together of an evening. We believe the Lord has entrusted their education to us, but there are only twenty-four hours in a day. My wife's strength has waned since the twins came, and even more so recently. You'll probably notice when you see her. Most of the housework is left to Hannah until Susanna's condition improves. I wanted to tell you personally, so that you don't think me ungrateful for your offer to teach the children. We can only spare the two children who aren't old enough to work a full day. You understand?"

"I do."

"Go on inside. Wade and Doris will be happy to learn whatever you wish to teach them. I have to get back to my trees."

"Thank you, sir." Olivia hesitated at the door, hoping Susanna Vestal would receive her as kindly as Christopher had.

She turned the knob and called out before she stepped inside. "Hello?"

"Mind your footing," a young voice cautioned from the kitchen. "It's washday."

Olivia stepped through the mudroom, up two creaky steps, and into the kitchen. Two tubs, one with soapy water and one with clear water, were on the floor next to the range. A kettle whistled on the stovetop, and fourteen-year-old Hannah lifted it with a folded dishtowel. "Careful through the puddles."

Olivia skirted the tubs. "So sorry to bother your work."

"No bother. With twins washday comes twice a week." Hannah blew a strand of light brown hair off her face as she poured the steaming water into a pot of pre-soaked diapers. "Mother is putting the twins down for their nap upstairs. Wade and Doris have a surprise for you. They saw you walking to the house with Father and are waiting in the parlor. Go in."

Olivia tiptoed across the wet kitchen floor and into the slim front room the Vestals were calling a parlor. The two children had arranged footstools for seats and a trunk as a desk. Wade held an open palm to a ledger-sized blackboard on an easel made of sticks.

Little Doris clapped her fingertips excitedly. "It's for you, Miss Owens! This is our classroom."

"How lovely! And I have something for each of you." Olivia opened her satchel and produced a reader for each of the children and a copy of *The New England Primer* for them to share.

They sat on their footstools, attentive and eager, while Olivia read to them. As she taught, the monster never once threatened to blind her from the page. Letters clearly formed words and the words formed sentences. And as quickly as her vision passed over the words, her mouth formed their sounds.

Mid-afternoon, as the children read silently, Mrs. Vestal descended the stairs. She stepped with such careful incremental movements that Olivia first thought the twins must have still been napping. But when Susanna reached the bottom of the narrow staircase she stopped and steadied herself with both hands on the wall. She breathed heavily with an open mouth.

Olivia rushed to her. "Mrs. Vestal, are you all right?"

Susanna gazed up with bloodshot eyes. "Don't alarm the children."

"I'm sorry," she whispered as she took in Susanna's willowy form and ashen skin. "I will run and get Doctor Ashton."

"No." Susanna grabbed her arm with a weak grip. "There isn't anything he can do."

Olivia glanced back into the parlor at Wade and Doris. They were absorbed in their reading. She lowered her voice. "Would you like me to call Mr. Vestal inside?"

"No."

"Do you have any medicine for your illness?"

"There is no remedy for my condition." Susanna peeled her hands from the wall. "There is nothing that can be done for me."

Olivia swallowed hard. "Mrs. Vestal, I'm so sorry. I didn't know you were ill."

"No one knows, except Christopher and Doctor Ashton," she pressed a palm to her middle, "and I want to keep it that way. Christopher and I are trusting God to heal me."

"Is there anything I can do?"

Susanna looked at her with pain-filled eyes. "Pray for my comfort. And for the children should the Lord choose to heal me through death."

CHAPTER FIVE

Olivia rubbed her throbbing temples and checked the time on the Ashtons' mantel clock again. The rhythmic banging of Gabe's hammer resounded through the timber wall of the Ashtons' kitchen as he helped the doctor and his four sons finish the addition to the house.

The pounding didn't distract little Sarah Ashton. She'd either grown used to the construction noise or had nerves of iron. The latter seemed unlikely for an eight-year-old, even an Ashton.

This was Olivia's last home to teach in for the week, and she hoped to finish Sarah's lessons before the men began cutting the hole in the wall for the doorway into the new rooms.

Sitting beside Sarah at the rectangular kitchen table, Olivia flipped the Bible's page as her pupil continued copying The Ten Commandments. Sarah's pencil slowly stroked her tablet for several minutes unabated.

The hammering stopped. Sarah paused her writing, mid-commandment. She smiled an adorable missing-tooth grin. "They must be done!"

Olivia tapped the page. "Finish your copy work. I'll go check."

"Our house is going to be twice as big as it is now."

"That will be very nice for you and your family."

Before Olivia reached the front door, it opened. The Ashton men filed into the kitchen, laughing about some construction mishap they had barely avoided. Doctor Ashton wore flannel and suspenders and walked with a slight limp. His trimmed gray beard framed his contented grin as he and Jonah carried saws and hatchets into the house.

Gabe followed them with his hammer in his hand. When his eyes met Olivia's, he gave her a sly quarter smile.

Something stirred inside her and left her feeling vulnerable. She inwardly rebuked the unwelcome sensation and returned her attention to Sarah's copy work. "*Thou shalt not steal...* you may stop at the word *steal* for now. Begin with verse sixteen on your own tomorrow. We will ask your father if you can use the family Bible this week. I must take mine home with me."

"I have my own Bible..." Sarah said something else too, but Olivia couldn't hear her over the men's voices. The air filled with the smell of sweat and sawdust as the Ashton men moved about the cramped room, discussing their plan for cutting the doorway.

Olivia closed her Bible and slid it into her satchel. She squatted to be eye-level with Sarah. "I enjoyed my time with you today. You are an excellent student. I look forward to teaching you again next week. Remember to do your copy work and practice your multiplication facts on your slate each day until our next lesson."

"I will, Olivia, er, Miss Owens."

She stood and smiled down at Sarah. Lifting the strap of her satchel to her shoulder, she got Doctor Ashton's attention. He met her at the open door. "Not staying to watch the demolition?"

"Demolition? I thought you were cutting a doorway into the new addition."

He winked. "That is my plan, but you never know what might happen with this crew!" He put a hand to her back as he walked outside with her. "How did Sarah do today?"

"Quite well. My mother always spoke of the Ashton intelligence, and I believe Sarah is continuing the tradition." She squinted from the bright noon sunlight. "I had hoped James would join us today."

Doctor Ashton nodded. "He has worked with Gabriel on the house addition from the beginning and was eager to help finish it. I will make sure he is at the table and ready for you next week."

"Thank you." Olivia took a step away then halted. "Doctor Ashton, may I ask you something?"

"Of course." He tilted his head. "What is it?"

She glanced behind him into the house. Gabe had hung a plumb line and was marking the wall. The others were gathered around him, ready with their chisels and mallets. Sarah was standing on a kitchen chair to watch. Still, Olivia kept her volume down. "It's about Mrs. Vestal."

"What about Susanna?"

"She isn't well. When I was at their house on Monday, she could barely walk down the stairs. Her skin was a sickly color and she looked very thin. She didn't tell me her exact condition, but I fear it is serious. She said you have seen her about it. Is there nothing to be done for her?"

"I cannot discuss a patient's condition with you." Doctor Ashton crossed his arms. "Do you believe she is in immediate danger?"

"I don't know, but you should go see her soon."

"Did Susanna ask you to tell me this?"

"No, but—"

"Did Christopher?"

"No."

Doctor Ashton drew a long breath. "Olivia, I understand you are concerned, and it's out of compassion that you want Susanna to have more medical attention, but her utmost concern at this stage is privacy. She and Christopher are hoping for a full recovery, and she doesn't want to be thought of as sickly."

"Can you at least tell me what is wrong with her?"

"I cannot."

"She said no one knows except for Mr. Vestal and you. If her situation is terminal, the community should know."

"I must abide by my patient's wishes. That is part of being a professional." Doctor Ashton scratched his bearded cheek. "At every turn in this school debate, I have voted in your favor. I have kept the matter of your reading difficulties private so they wouldn't deny you the chance to teach. Take care that you don't use your profession to spread private matters throughout the village. As people let you into their homes, you must understand they are not only trusting you with their children's education but also with their privacy. You must behave accordingly."

"If Susanna is dying, the church should be informed so they can pray for her. The ladies in the village should be given a chance to help her family, to take over what work they could, to comfort the Vestal children. The children should know if their mother is dying."

"Dear girl, we are all dying," he patted her arm to calm her, "but rarely do we live like it."

Olivia's shoulders slumped unable to bear the weight of a secret so heavy. Hot tears blurred her vision and she looked away.

He lifted her chin in the tender fatherly way he did when she was little and she went to him afraid the disappearing words meant something was wrong with her vision. Assurance filled his gentle voice now just as it had back then. "God will give you the strength you need for this. You might be the only woman Susanna Vestal trusts during this time. If she makes any requests of you, do your best to help her."

"I will."

Doctor Ashton nodded sympathetically. As he turned to walk back into his house, Gabe stepped outside. His gaze fell on Olivia, and his expression changed. He held up an ax and looked at Doctor Ashton. "I'm going to the workshop to sharpen this. Don't let your sons start hacking into that wall while I'm gone."

Olivia walked to the road while the doctor's chuckle rang out. She covertly wiped a tear from her cheek, hoping Gabe hadn't noticed.

Footsteps approached rapidly as he caught up to her. "Are you in a hurry to get to your next lesson?"

"No." The knot in her throat had yet to loosen. All she could think of was Mrs. Vestal's condition and the children. "I have to go home." Her voice cracked, betraying her sadness, but she barreled ahead.

Gabe kept up. "What's wrong, Liv?"

She shook her head. "I can't say."

"You can tell me."

"No, I can't. I'm not allowed."

He breathed deeply as if he were about to speak. She almost faced him but didn't want him to see her red eyes. She shifted the weight of her book-filled satchel and immediately felt a hand under the strap.

Gabe lifted it from her shoulder.

"That's a first." His voice warmed.

The inviting tone made her angle her chin toward him. "What is?"

"Letting me carry your books."

"I don't recall you ever trying before."

"I'm sure I tried when we were in school."

"No. I would remember that."

"Hm." Gabe drew his head back a degree. "I didn't?"

"No."

"Well, I should have. I know I wanted to."

"No need to apologize. As I recall you were too busy teasing us girls to bother with chivalry."

He laughed easily. "Yes, when we were very young, that was true, but not once we were older. In fact, I remember wanting to carry your books and walk you home during my last year of school, but you were usually too pensive and prickly to get near."

She grinned at his accurate description. Years of hiding her word blindness and listening to Peggy Cotter tell her the boys mocked her probably had made her prickly. Now as a teacher, it was even more important that she hide her impairment. And she wasn't so sure she could believe Peggy's commentary anymore, but she could try to ignore it for the sake of friendship.

Those things might never change, yet Gabe had the ability to make her feel better in a few minutes after she had endured a week of difficulty. She glanced up at him. "I am sorry. My prickles were not intended to hurt you."

"Nor was my teasing." He caught her eye. "Whatever happened today at the Ashtons', I want to help."

As they walked along the road, the thick foliage of the tall and sturdy gray leaf trees blocked the sun. "That is kind of you, but nothing happened today. The Ashtons are wonderful."

Gabe's brow knit in concentration. "Then perhaps you are dreading wherever you must go to teach next. Are you off to the Colburns' or the Fosters' this afternoon?"

"Neither. I'm keeping Thursday afternoons open for the Colburns, but for now they want to teach their children themselves. And Benjamin wants to be in the pasture with his father, so I'm not going to the Fosters' house either."

"Then was it something your family did yesterday?" he asked.

She shook her head. "My siblings' lessons were the easiest so far, probably because I know what to expect with them.

Except Richie kept playing with our mother's freshly sharpened sewing scissors."

Gabe chortled. "Yes, what is Richie's fascination with cutting things?"

Olivia shrugged. "Maybe it's a case of *boys will be boys*?"

"Fair enough," Gabe said, returning to his investigation in the lighthearted way that drew her in. "Did something happen at the Roberts' house Tuesday morning or with my family that afternoon? Did my naughty siblings hurt your feelings?"

"No, no. Although, it sounds as if you have been tracking my movement through the village."

"I have committed your teaching schedule to memory." He hooked his thumb in the strap of the satchel and smiled. "I thought if I caught you between lessons, you would let me carry your books. It is my contribution to the furtherance of formal education in the settlement of Good Springs."

She laughed at his goofy grin. "You are ridiculous."

"And now you are teasing me."

"I'm sorry. I suppose I still have my prickles. It's been a trying week. And not just in one way. There are many... problems."

"I care about you, Liv. I don't want to see you upset." Gabe stopped walking. "If you can't tell me what that was about with Doctor Ashton, can you tell me about the other difficulties?"

Olivia hummed an exhalation and glanced around. There weren't any people in sight. A jackrabbit scampered into the forest. She watched it in the distance behind Gabe. "Where do I start? Some of the students have forgotten what little arithmetic they knew. I had an eight-year-old who couldn't tell me how many were in a dozen and a seven-year-old who thought the number 4 was a letter." Her hand fluttered in frustration. "I wouldn't mind all the review lessons, but some parents see our isolation as proof the children only need to learn practical skills. One mother told me not to muddle up her child's brain with unnecessary subjects like Geography and Algebra."

She took a slow breath as Gabe listened. His attentiveness tempted her to mention her concern with the Cotters and the Vestals, but Doctor Ashton had admonished her not to speak of families' private matters. "This village needs a dedicated schoolhouse, so that the students can focus. Right now they are distracted by chores and their parents and..." As her agitation mounted, her hand gestures grew. "I am distracted by their parents. I truly believe this settlement will be a flourishing society someday. We will need formally educated citizens. Even though most of the adults here were educated in America, no one seems to care anymore."

Gabe took the hand she was waving. He held her fingers firmly in his broad palm. "I care."

"Then will you tell the elders to set aside land and build a schoolhouse for me?"

His eyes searched her face, but for what she didn't know. "I can't. You know the rules. Everyone is supposed to take concerns in regard to any settlement business to their family elder. Since your elder is still your father, it's up to him to decide how to handle it or take it to the elders."

She yanked her hand away from his gentle grip. "What do you mean since my elder is still my father? How could that change?"

Gabe moved close and lowered his voice to a near whisper. "If a woman marries an elder, he would become her spokesman to the elder council."

"How does that apply to me? The village elders are all married men, most of them over forty, all with several children. I would never marry one of them!"

"I didn't mean you should marry a current elder." Gabe groaned. "If you were to marry a firstborn son, who would inherit his father's position, he could speak for your interests in elder meetings."

"That is ludicrous! I'm not going to marry, let alone for the sake of having my concerns heard by a husband instead of a father."

He patted the air with a placating hand. "I'm not saying you should. You asked how to change your elder, so I told you how you could change. It was hypothetical."

"Forget hypothetical. Since my father won't help me get a schoolhouse built, I should change things myself."

"What do you mean?"

"I could go to Reverend Colburn personally." Olivia pointed at her satchel and he slid the strap off his shoulder and passed it to her. "I could prepare a convincing argument and persuade him to authorize the schoolhouse."

"It wouldn't do any good. The elders decide on land and building issues together."

The breeze picked up and tossed a strand of Olivia's hair across her face. Before she could move it off, Gabe traced it behind her ear. His caring touch felt sincere no matter what Peggy had said about his flirtatious ways. Maybe that was it: maybe his blithe attitude and inclination to touch combined to give the impression of insincerity when he had actually grown into a caring man who would one day become a village elder.

…one day become a village elder.

He had suggested she marry a man who would one day inherit his father's position on the elder council to give her more influence in the village decisions. Surely he hadn't meant himself. If he had, was he teasing her? Testing her? Since she hadn't swooned when he flirted, had he thought hinting at marriage would stir a discernable reaction? It hadn't.

Or was he simply saying marriage is one way to change her situation?

Regardless of his meaning or motive, she would not respond. He was standing inches from her, gazing down at her with eyes so clear she wondered if she looked long enough she might see his soul. A dark blue circle outlined his crystalline irises. She'd never noticed that before. The brown of his lashes was a shade darker than his eyebrows. She hadn't noticed that before either.

His gaze was set on her as deeply as hers was on him. "Sundown tonight," he said.

"Pardon?"

"The Ashtons are babysitting for Jonah and Marian this evening so we can go to the shore and have a campfire like we used to. The moon will be full. Mr. Weathermon believes it will be the last clear night for a while."

"Oh," Olivia's cheeks heated.

Gabe squinted slightly and smirked. "What did you think I meant?"

"No, I... didn't think anything," she lied. "Yes, a campfire with friends. That sounds like... exactly what I need."

"Good." He pointed a thumb to the west. "The elders have given me the land I wanted. It runs from behind Jonah's property all the way to the big stream. I'm going to clear the area nearest Mr. Weathermon's cabin to build a house soon. The men volunteered to take turns giving up a morning of their work to help me clear land and hew the logs. They want to finish before winter, so I probably won't see you around the village for a while. I was hoping you would come to the beach tonight." He pointed his ax at the workshop. "I have to sharpen this and get back to work. I could come to your house before sundown and walk you to the shore if you like. Henry can go ahead for us and build the fire."

"Has anyone invited Peggy yet?"

He shrugged one shoulder.

She hoped his indifference was sincere. Still, Peggy was her friend. "I will go to her house this afternoon and tell her about the campfire. She hates walking to the beach alone, so she will want to walk with me. But thank you for your offer." She adjusted the strap of her satchel. "We will meet you there at sundown... like old times."

"Old times..." Gabe rubbed his thumb along the ax's handle. "I hope not."

CHAPTER SIX

O livia straightened the buttoned cuffs at her wrists as she
hiked along the sandy path to the shore. She'd spent the
afternoon mending the hem on her day dress, washing her hair,
and practicing ladylike postures in the mirror. And now,
walking beside the spring-curled Peggy Cotter to the beach,
she felt like a drab schoolteacher.

And sand was leaking into her boots.

Peggy's cuffs were ruffled layers of elegant lace. She'd
spent the last ten minutes boring Olivia with every detail of
their intricate stitching. The corset Peggy wasn't supposed to
be wearing unnaturally shaped her posture, forcing her bosom
forward and her rump backward like a queen bee.

As they approached the beach, the fading daylight
confirmed a finely ground starch concoction hid the blemishes
on Peggy's chin. Olivia felt foolish for even trying to primp for
the evening. One look at Peggy and Gabriel McIntosh would
forget Olivia existed.

That was for the best. She had no business hoping for his
attention. She'd never fallen in love in her life. Perhaps her
cold heart was simply incapable. Regardless, she'd wasted an
afternoon thinking a little effort on her part might make her

look like other women. It didn't matter because there was no chance she would be like other women.

She'd also hoped the ten-minute walk to the shore would provide her with an opportunity to ask Peggy about Mrs. Cotter's rude behavior. The roar of the breaking waves grew louder as they closed in on the shore, and her chance was slipping away. As they neared the end of the path through the whistling tussock grass, Peggy finally ended her discourse on the nuances of lacemaking with, "...which is why I would never use the thread made from Mrs. Roberts' silk fibers."

Olivia sighed. "Eventually, you will run out of the thread you brought to this land, and you will be glad Mrs. Roberts knows how to keep silkworms."

They passed the cairn that marked the place where the settlers first came ashore. Beyond the stone pillar, three log benches encircled a cone-shaped pile of wood and sticks. A wisp of smoke rose from its center as Gabe and Jonah stoked the campfire to life.

Marian was between the campfire and the waterline, gathering seashells. Her silky blond hair was pinned back on one side, exposing her ear, and tumbled down her back in golden layers. When she spotted Olivia, she waved with vigorous enthusiasm and hurried toward her.

Peggy shielded her mouth with her gloved hand. "Goodness, what a ninny!"

Olivia flashed Peggy a scolding stare, raised the front of her dress, and ran to meet her dearest friend with equal exuberance. Marian welcomed her with a warm embrace, then linked arms with her like they did when they were schoolgirls. Olivia glanced back at Peggy. She was nearing the campfire, sashaying for Gabe's attention.

"Don't worry about her," Marian said. "Let's look for pretty shells before we lose the last light of day."

Olivia tightened her shawl around her shoulders. "I should say hello to Gabriel and Jonah first."

"We will just be a moment. It's almost dark. This is my first time away from home without the baby, and I intend to enjoy it."

The youthful energy of Marian's happiness stirred something in Olivia—something she thought was gone. "All right." She cast her gaze across the darkening ocean. "Just for a moment."

As they strode farther from the growing campfire, Olivia scanned the tide-flattened beach for shells. The black point of a shark's tooth protruded from the sand. She plucked it out and handed it to Marian. "Do you still collect these?"

"Oh, yes. Thank you." Marian slipped it into the pocket of her lavender dress then picked up a tiny clamshell. "Look how little this is. Must have been a baby. I wonder how my Frederick is doing with his grandparents right now."

Olivia smiled at her. "He couldn't be in more capable hands."

"You're right." Marian slipped the miniature shell into her pocket. "I'm always with him, and if I'm not, I'm thinking about him."

"I've heard that new mothers fall in love with their babies just as powerfully as they did with their husbands. Is it true?"

Now it was Marian who smiled. "I suppose that depends on the woman and her relationship with her husband. I'm certainly in love with them both—Jonah and Frederick. It's two different loves, but equal in magnetism. I'm enjoying my evening out, but it's all I can do not to run back to the Ashtons' house to see my baby."

"Ah, then I shall keep you occupied." A scattering of coral beads caught Olivia's eye. After a quick survey of the fading daylight, she pointed at the multi-colored bits of coral. "Let's get a few of these and then go back. They have the fire going, and you probably want to spare Jonah from Peggy's flirtation."

"She doesn't try that with him anymore, and if she did, Jonah knows how to handle her." Marian's gaze fell on the coral beads, and her eyes widened. "Oh, these are pretty! They would make a lovely bracelet, don't you think?"

Olivia heard Marian's words, but her attention was fixed on Peggy and Gabe. He squatted near the fire with a poker stick in hand, while Peggy stood upwind of him, no doubt hoping her feminine scent would draw him from his fire stoking. Her lips moved with incessant chatter. Lord only knew what she was saying to him. Or how he would respond. Why hadn't he responded yet?

"Olivia?"

She snapped her attention away from Peggy and Gabe. "Pardon?"

Marian erected her posture and glanced over Olivia's shoulder. "Try as she may, Gabriel is not interested in her."

"That isn't the way she tells it."

"I know what Gabriel wants and it's not Peggy Cotter. Forget what she says," Marian held out a fistful of coral pieces, "and watch what she does."

Peggy was trying to get Gabe's attention, but he didn't give it. Olivia thought back. It often looked like that, though in private Peggy insisted otherwise. Maybe Marian was right. She did know Gabe better these days since he and her husband were close friends.

Olivia accepted the beads. "Don't you want to make a bracelet out of these?"

"You should have them. Make a necklace. The colors will look beautiful against your skin."

"Not that it would matter on a schoolteacher."

"What does that mean? Why shouldn't a teacher have pretty things?" Marian brushed the sand from her palms and continued without giving her a chance for rebuttal. "You have been listening to Peggy too much. Has nothing changed since our schooldays?"

"I don't know."

"Peggy always wanted all the boys' attention. If Gabriel paid you any mind, Peggy would berate you in her cunning

I'm-doing-this-for-your-own-good way. Does she still do that?"

"Sometimes. But she's only trying to protect me."

"You don't still believe that, do you?" Marian clicked her tongue. "She is the only other woman in the settlement our age. We will have to deal with her schemes all our lives if she doesn't change. And yes, she is our friend and there are times when she means well, but don't let her lies blind you to what God has for you. It's time to see each other as adults. We aren't thirteen anymore."

The blunt summation of her relationships cut sharper than Peggy's criticism, but it wasn't Marian's fault. Olivia glanced back at the campfire. Gabe was gathering sticks, and Peggy was coyly swishing her skirt as she followed him through the sandy grass, chatting.

Olivia stood still. Her mind froze while childhood whirled past on one side and adulthood stalled on the other. She'd wanted the elders to see her as a grown woman, and yet she still saw her peers as if they were adolescents. But how could she move past schoolyard attitudes if Peggy was whispering lies to her?

In an isolated settlement every relationship was important. She wouldn't destroy one of her few friendships over this. But Marian was right: things had to change.

Her eyes lost focus as she stared at the movement around the campfire. "Peggy has a way of convincing me. She says Gabe is only kind to my face, but he laughs about me later."

Marian shook her head. "Never."

"What about when we were—"

"Thirteen?"

"Well… yes."

"Are you still sore about that? Boys tease girls. It happened to all of us."

Olivia remembered their school years differently. Hers was a daily battle against an invisible monster, and she had decided it was better not to be intimately known than to be known and mocked. Even now she couldn't fully explain her sensitivity without giving away her secret. "I guess he picked the wrong days to tease me and it stuck with me."

Marian touched her arm. "We have all changed."

"Yes, and Peggy says Gabe is now just a tomcat."

"Gabriel McIntosh has grown into a charming, but honest man. He lives beyond himself, which is more than I can say for Peggy." Marian motioned toward the village. "Look at all that he has helped build. And there have been days when he has worked from sunrise to sunset and then he goes with Jonah to check on Mr. Weathermon."

"But he still jokes around a lot too."

"Sometimes a sense of humor can lighten the heaviest woes."

It was true and she'd often benefitted in spirit from Gabe's desire to lift her mood. He was charming, but wasn't charm deceptive? "He can be so flirtatious."

"He's personable with everyone, but flirtatious?" A smile curved the edge of Marian's mouth. "Only with you."

A twinge of regret gnawed inside her. "And here I've made a habit of cutting him short because Peggy says he is like that with all the girls."

"You must ignore Peggy. Before Jonah and I were married, she swore he was intrigued with her. He wasn't then, and Gabriel isn't now. Henry was the only man who ever liked her, poor fellow, and he's even grown to see past her pretty face. What he discovered beneath was not the godly woman he hoped to find. Are you going to keep your confidence in Peggy's lies, or see her for who she is?"

Olivia watched Peggy and Gabe as Henry arrived at the campfire. Gabe thrust his hand forward, and Henry shook it. Peggy immediately flung herself between them and spread her hands on Henry's lapels. Her behavior did seem contrary to her claim that she had no romantic interest in Henry.

At once, Olivia saw them as they were. Gabe was not the insatiable flirt. Peggy was.

Gabe had said he hoped their gathering tonight was not like old times. Maybe this was what he meant.

His insightfulness stunned her. It wouldn't be the first time others saw something she could not. She couldn't stop the monster from blinding her to words, but she could stop Peggy from blinding her to Gabe.

"No. I won't listen to her." Olivia stepped closer to Marian. "Not anymore."

"I'm glad to hear it. So taking Peggy's schemes out of the equation, what do you see between you and Gabriel?"

Good question. If his kind words and tender affections had been sincere, she might believe he was in love with her. If so, was she capable of falling in love? Was that what she wanted?

He had plenty of admirable qualities, but to allow him to truly love her would require him to know her completely. That felt too risky. She could ignore Peggy's lies and accept Gabe as sincere, but she couldn't give herself permission to fall in love. Not the kind of love that brought marriage and babies and not being able to leave the house without yearning to be back home with said husband and babies. Not yet. Not without building the trusting relationship that sort of life depended upon.

"Well?" Marian asked, waiting for her answer. "What do you see between you and Gabriel?"

She dropped her shoulders. "I think he might admire me."

Marian raised her eyebrows, scrunching the flawless skin of her forehead. "You *think*?"

"Yes. Maybe. He has said some sweet things—"

"What did he say? I want to hear every word!" Marian tapped her fingertips together and emitted a short squeal. "I've been waiting a long time for this!"

Olivia rolled her eyes, but a smile broke her affectation. "Oh, all right. Last week when he walked me home from your house, I asked him if I could count on his loyalty in friendship, and he said that I had it and so much more if only I would let him."

"That's promising." Marian nodded briskly. "And what else?"

"This afternoon, he wanted to help me."

"With what?"

"He saw that I was upset and he wanted to fix it. Not fix it as he would with a broken piece of furniture, but he wanted to come to my aid. He said he cares about me. It wasn't just what he said but how he looked when he said it. And he notices the smallest details about me. I know that doesn't mean he is in love with me—"

"Oh, but he is! He has been for so long, but you never showed any interest. Jonah said you never would come around, but I knew you would." Marian beamed. "It appears my husband owes me a dollar."

"You can't mean it."

"Of course not. His money is no good here." Marian waved her hand vigorously. "Never mind that. Gabriel has been in love with you for years. The question is how do you feel about him?"

"I don't know."

Marian hooked an arm through hers. "Will you tell me when you do know?"

"Of course. You're my dearest friend," she said as they started walking toward the campfire, arms linked. "Your opinion matters more to me than any other. If you say he is trustworthy, then I will give him a chance."

Marian raised her chin. "That is all I ask," she said with an exaggerated formal tone, and they both laughed.

When near the fire, one by one each of the others turned to look at them. A flash of jealousy moved across Peggy's face, and she stepped closer to Henry. He stepped away. Jonah walked toward Marian, possessive pride igniting his grin.

Gabe caught Olivia's gaze and held it. The last light in the western sky faded behind him and the fire highlighted his profile. He lowered the handful of kindling to his side. His hands were always holding something—a hammer, an ax, kindling—but could she trust them to hold her heart?

She felt Marian release her arm and heard her and Jonah exchange sweet whispers, but all she could focus on was the man standing before her. As she moved into the circle of log benches, a comfortable grin warmed his expression. Her feet walked toward him even as her mind cautioned each step.

He held an open palm to the bench beside him. "I saved you a seat."

"How thoughtful."

"I'm always thinking of—" He briefly glanced away.

Jonah and Marian were mid-smooch. Peggy was trying to figure out how to sit elegantly on a log while wearing a corset. Henry was shaving the bark off a gray leaf stick with his pocketknife. No one was paying them any attention. So why had Gabe stopped himself?

Olivia sat on the bench. "Thinking of what?"

He tossed the kindling to the sand near the campfire and lowered himself to the bench beside her. "I was going to say that I'm always thinking of you, because it's true, but last time I said that, it offended you."

"You said you hoped tonight was not like old times. I agree."

He was close enough to block the ocean wind, but not close enough to make her uncomfortable in front of the others. She shifted to face him squarely. "If your thoughtfulness is sincere, I've been a fool to be offended by it."

"I am sincere, Liv." Concern marked his brow. "I do care about you. And you are no fool."

The others had gone quiet. Olivia felt their watching eyes and hoped no one had heard his sweet words. If only they could go somewhere to talk alone.

Jonah flashed a crooked smile at Gabe. "Tell the girls what you and Mr. Weathermon caught in the stream last week."

Gabe leaned forward, bracing his elbows on his knees. "We caught a shark."

Olivia felt her jaw fall open.

"A shark?" Marian gasped.

Peggy put her hand to her bosom. "In the big stream? Where the children swim in the summertime?"

Gabe nodded. "We've seen them in the estuary south of the settlement before, but this one ventured upstream."

Marian drew her head back. "How big was it?"

Gabe spread his palms wide, one hand coming in front of Olivia. "It was just a baby. Still big enough to bite a man's hand off if it wanted to. Or a woman's."

Marian's eyes widened. Peggy gave a dramatic shiver. Henry and Jonah laughed at the ladies' adverse reaction.

As Gabe recounted the details of helping Mr. Weathermon get the shark off his fishing line, he took Olivia's fingertips in his hand. He didn't look at her or draw attention to the simple gesture. He kept his lively story animated with enough detail to make the women squirm and the men comment as if they had witnessed the event themselves.

Olivia tried to listen, to focus on his words and their friends, but as she sat there, fingers covertly entwined with his, her thoughts blurred. This man sincerely cared for her. She searched her heart and found confirmation she cared for him too. But she wasn't in love, at least not how other women described the feeling. Why couldn't she be a normal woman?

Why had she suddenly allowed this to matter? It didn't matter whether she was capable of falling in love or not because she'd sworn never to allow it. She was devoted to teaching children, not making them. But it wasn't her mission to teach that forced her to be different. She was different. She had an inexplicable flaw, and just as Doctor Ashton had told her when she was young, people didn't accept what they couldn't understand. The thorn in her side would have to remain hidden.

If she allowed Gabe to court her, it might lead to marriage. Wasn't that the point of courting? If she married, he'd find out about the word blindness. Or she'd have to tell him. What if it was something that could be passed on to their children? The mental imagine of a cabin full of fussy, word blind children made her cringe. There she was in the middle of a cramped kitchen, sweating over a stove, explaining to her disappointed husband that he'd married a defective woman and now he had a house full of defective children.

Their children. She shook her head at the thought. One touch from a man who cared about her and she was contemplating having a family with him. She was getting ahead of herself.

She had to slow her thoughts down. He cared about her, and she liked him enough to give him a chance. That's all. She knew how to keep the thorn in her side hidden.

Sitting there, beneath the oval moon, skin touching skin, her self-deprecating thoughts churned as violently as the fierce ocean nearby. The torrent clouded her mind. The only thing she knew for certain was that if she tried to read a page right now there was no way she would be able to see the words. But it didn't matter. For now she didn't have to read or learn or label anything. She only had to allow her heart to consider something it never had.

CHAPTER SEVEN

No, Richie, come back with that!" Olivia yelled at her nine-year-old brother as he sneaked away from the kitchen table. When he complied, she pulled their mother's sewing scissors from his hand and closed the blades. "You must stop playing with scissors. You have already ruined Alice's ribbons and Walter's suspenders. I dare not think what else."

Richie wrinkled his freckled nose. "I like cutting things."

"When you are done with your schoolwork, ask Father's permission to use the old shears and cut something productive out-of-doors." She patted the back of the kitchen chair where he was supposed to be sitting. "But you aren't leaving the table again until you finish your equations."

Across the wooden table, Martha eyed her. Boredom flattened Martha's face. "Maybe he is drawn to sharp objects because these lessons are so dull."

"That's very clever, Martha." Olivia flicked her youngest sister a scowl and opened a grammar book. "Since you're so fond of wordplay, copy these two pages of verbs in simple present tense and write the correct past participle form beside each word."

Almeda snickered at Martha's assignment until her gaze met Olivia's. She tucked her chin and returned to her essay writing. The sound of pencils scratching paper whispered through the Owenses' kitchen. Their lesson time might end productively after all.

In haste to start her day, Olivia had left her silver watch pin upstairs. She didn't need a clock to know when it was noon. Her siblings, like all of her students, could be depended on to exuberantly announce when class time was over. Then they would scatter from the table as if sitting there to write one more answer would bring on boils. The settlement's children only had class one half-day per week and complained for most of it, except some of the younger ones like Jane Cotter, Sarah Ashton, and Doris Vestal. In only four weeks of teaching, Olivia knew who her favorite pupils would be.

While Almeda, Martha, and Richie worked on their assignments, Olivia paced to the back door. She tried not to take it personally when students complained about their assignments. They didn't know how hard she had to work to prepare lessons. Most of them had heard their parents complain about schoolwork taking up time, and so they complained too.

Teaching from house to house was only reinforcing the opinion that formal education was an imposition. And that attitude reinforced her opinion that it would take a dedicated schoolhouse and a habit of daily class times to build respect for education in the settlement.

She had left the matter alone for nearly a month while teaching in homes and allowing the children to adjust to having her as their schoolteacher. Gazing through the circular window in the back door, she watched her father and Walter traipse toward the house for lunch. It was time to resume her cause. She wiped a smudge from the former porthole glass and steeled herself for her next battle.

As soon as the first boot step hit the porch, Richie sprang from his seat. "They're home! It's noon!"

"We're done with school!" Almeda sang.

Martha clapped her book shut. "Hallelujah, we are saved."

Footsteps thudded up the staircase as the children raced to put away their schoolbooks. Olivia rolled her eyes. "Class dismissed." Her deflated mumble was lost on the empty room.

Richard Sr. opened the back door, but stayed outside while he removed his muddy boots. "Have you got lunch together yet, Livy?"

She shook her head. "I just finished teaching. Mother said she would make lunch when she came back from the coop."

Richard furrowed his brow. "What is she doing out there?"

"Checking the wire. A hen was missing again today."

Walter squeezed past their father. "At least the cow has milk again."

Before her brother made it inside, Richard pulled on his arm. "Fetch a pail of water from the well, son."

"Yes, sir." Walter grabbed an empty bucket and jumped from the porch.

"He's eager to please today." Olivia glanced at her father as she reached into the cabinet beside the door. "He must have enjoyed clearing land for Gabriel this morning."

Richard stepped inside, looking more pleasant than usual. "The building site is cleared. Has been for a week. We were hewing lumber for the house today."

She missed seeing Gabe around the village. His land wasn't visible from the road, and he hadn't been at the McIntosh house when she taught there. She only saw him at church on Sundays, and then his younger siblings vied for his attention. They had missed him all week too.

Though she had mentioned his handholding to Marian, no one else seemed the wiser about his sweet gesture. Many times since the campfire on the beach she'd recalled the warmth of having her hand in his. Maybe one day they would spend more time together, maybe not, but for now the memory of his affection gave her a spark of happiness on otherwise dreary days. Recalling his touch was insidiously impractical, but undeniably delightful.

She snapped herself from her reverie and peeled back the tea towel covering the breadbasket. "There is plenty of bread for lunch, Father. I'll make biscuits in the Dutch to go with dinner."

"Sounds good." Richard flashed a rare grin. "Gabriel spoke to me this morning."

She paused as she drew tin plates from the cupboard. "Spoke to you? I should imagine he speaks to everyone who helps with the work on his house."

"This was about you."

"Oh." She carried the stack of plates to the table. Her brothers and sisters would return any moment. She didn't know if Gabe planned to further their relationship and certainly didn't want anyone else knowing, at least not yet. "Quickly then. What did he say?"

Richard eyed the staircase, seeming to understand her urgency. "He asked for my blessing."

"To marry me?" A plate slipped as she lowered the stack to table. She jumped at the dull clank of tin. "That's a little premature."

Richard steadied her with a fatherly hand. It was the most attention he'd paid her in months. "He admires you and needed to state his intentions to me."

"How very presumptuous."

"Very honorable, more like. It's the right thing to do between men. Gabriel understands these things, and I respect him for it. He will make a good husband for you."

Gabe had said he cared about her, and she'd decided to accept his compliments as sincere. They had shared one sweet moment four weeks ago. It led her to daydream what-ifs, but that was a long way from marriage. Maybe her father had misunderstood Gabriel's gregarious nature. "Did he actually say he is planning to propose marriage?"

Richard gave the light chuckle of a father amused by his naïve daughter. "He didn't have to. He is building a house. Bachelors don't build multiple-room homes, they build one-room cabins."

"We aren't courting."

"You didn't think he planned to live there alone, did you?"

"I hadn't thought about it. I admire him. He cares for me, but we have no further understanding between us. We are both occupied with our work. There simply isn't time for more." Not to mention she didn't want to marry unless she was in love—whatever that meant—and he wouldn't want her if he knew about her impairment anyway.

She traced a finger around and around the edge of the tin lunch plates. So many worries wrestled for her attention. Someone or something was stealing from them. She had to shoulder complaints about lessons from students and parents, dodge Mrs. Cotter's impolite behavior, and teach the Vestal children while Susanna lay ill and the twins ran Hannah ragged. Then, whenever the monster allowed her to see the written word, she had to customize her lesson plans for the inconvenient teaching arrangement she'd been forced into. The last thing she wanted was to take care of a husband and have his babies. Not now and maybe not ever.

She had given Gabriel McIntosh a cup, and he wanted a gallon.

And she couldn't be bothered with the distraction. "I can't think about marriage right now. Gabe can build his big home, but if he wants to build anything for me, it should be a schoolhouse."

"Not that again." Richard groaned, and his usual petulance returned. "I thought you would be happy that a man wants to marry you. You could have a family of your own."

"I don't see the point in making more children when the village refuses to prioritize educating the ones we have. Please mention building a schoolhouse during the elder meeting tonight."

Foot beats pattered the stairs as her siblings came back down. The back door opened, and Walter set a pail of water on the floor. Their mother was behind him with a sour expression.

Richard shook his head at Olivia. "I wholeheartedly gave him my blessing. I don't see how you could want for more."

* * *

Olivia waited until nine o'clock, hoping that would give the men enough time in their elder meeting to finish their pertinent business. Though not so much time that they would be too tired to hear her plea.

Under the pall of night, she slipped out the kitchen door and onto the road. After a glance back at her family's home, she tightened her shawl and hurried to the moonlit chapel. She should have prepared a formal speech to ensure she used all the modes of persuasion. Her passion for education had driven her this far, and she would have to rely on it to evoke emotion, establish credibility, and appeal to the logic of the village elders.

Even though it had done nothing to persuade her father.

She was alone in the darkness of night while all the other women were in their homes, mending or reading by lamplight. Children were tucked in their cozy beds. The elders were behind the closed doors of the chapel, making decisions that affected everyone else.

The road's sandy gravel crunched beneath her boots no matter how nimbly she stepped. As she passed the path to Jonah and Marian's house, the scamper of some small creature startled her. Twigs crackled in the blackened brush. Her eyes darted from one side of the road to the other, and she picked up her pace.

The cold evening air carried the scent of rain, but the moon was still visible between passing clouds. As she climbed the stone steps to the chapel, she turned back to check the sky to the east over the ocean. Lightning flickered in the distance.

Though the water couldn't be seen for the gray leaf trees, virescent light pulsed beneath the clouds. She had an hour at most until the storm rolled ashore.

Before Olivia gripped the door handle, she raised her heels and peeked through the narrow window in the arched door. Made from the planks of the *Providence*, the heavy wooden door still smelled like the sea and sweat and fear. Perhaps the stench of fear wasn't coming from the wood.

She shouldn't be here.

The isolated settlement had few rules and no formal government, but if the village had an unwritten law it was this: women should never enter a meeting of the village elders.

It hadn't mattered to her until her problem went unaddressed by the all-male elder council. Now she found their rule primitive and misogynistic. If they simply wanted one representative from each family, they could make the rule state the eldest child would inherit the position. Of course, that would only glorify age over gender, but then she would be in training to be the next representative for her family. She would be included in the meetings instead of being the girl at the door, dithering while grasping to justify her assertive plan.

Inside, the men were seated on the first two of the church's recently completed wooden pews. The lectern Reverend Colburn stood behind on Sunday mornings was in its place at the front of the chapel. Instead of standing behind the lectern, reading from his Bible, the reverend was standing beside it with one elbow leaning against it and his feet crossed at the ankle.

She surveyed the back of the other elders' heads and counted the men. Eleven total. The reverend, the seven other family elders including her father, and the three young men who would one day replace their fathers on the elder council—Jonah, Henry, and Gabriel—each sitting beside his father. They were all giving Mr. Roberts their attention. The reverend appeared to be focused on Mr. Roberts, but if he looked at the door he would see her peeking in.

She lowered her heels. Why did she have to do this? Her father should have taken up her cause. Why did she have to march into their meeting and demand their attention? Even Gabe could have done something before now. But he hadn't.

The children in this settlement—and all born after them—deserved an education. The elders had said so back when they planned the group migration, but she alone remembered. Her father had said teaching children was her calling no matter where she taught and she should focus on that. Her calling was indeed to the children, and they needed a schoolhouse and the daily routine of education to help them focus and feel stable.

Her father didn't care enough to take the matter before the elders. Gabe said he cared, but not enough to break the settlement's rules. It was up to her to stand up for the children.

She drew a long breath and turned the door handle. As she pulled the heavy door open, Reverend Colburn's eyes shot to her. He held up a finger, halting whatever Mr. Roberts was saying. One by one, the men turned their faces toward the door, the younger men agilely and the middle-aged men more stiffly. Within seconds all eyes were on her.

Her father stood. "Livy? What's wrong?" He managed to keep his voice inquisitive, but his scowl betrayed his anger. He knew why she was there. They all did.

She walked along the outside aisle to the front of the church. With every step forward, the empty click of her boot heels echoed off the chapel walls and ceiling. The hollow sound matched the worried expressions of the elders.

Reaching the front pew, she studied the faces of the men. She knew every one of them well, and they her, but her breach of custom made them feel like strangers. She opened her mouth to speak, but the unwelcoming stares frightened the words from her lips.

Doctor Ashton scratched his bearded cheek then shook his head with short rapid movement, warning her. Mr. Foster looked away. Even kind Mr. Vestal leaned his elbows upon his knees and watched her with one eyebrow raised.

Reverend Colburn broke the silence. "Yes, Miss Owens?"

"I've come to ask you all to consider my request. Jesus heard the appeals of those whom His disciples tried to turn away. I ask that you heed our Lord's example and hear me now."

Her father raked his callused fingers through his thinning hair. "I apologize for this, Reverend. Go home, Livy."

Reverend Colburn held up his hand, and her father slowly sat back down. The reverend returned his gaze to her. "What is your request?"

She had planned to look at each of the men one at a time to appeal to them individually as she addressed the group. But no matter how she tried, she couldn't look anyone in the eye other than Reverend Colburn. "As you know I've been teaching school from house to house for over a month. I am grateful for the honor of teaching the children, but one class per week is not sufficient to educate the next generation." She clasped her hands to keep from wringing them. "It is imperative that we build a schoolhouse and soon. The children will learn better in a dedicated environment and benefit greatly from the daily routine of a class schedule. Every man here received a proper education. The least we can do is offer the same opportunity to the children of Good Springs."

Reverend Colburn tapped one finger repeatedly on the lectern as he eyed her. She waited for him to harangue her for bypassing her family's elder, for disrespecting their rules, and for interrupting their meeting. At last, he broke his gaze and spread his palms toward the pews. "Does anyone want to sponsor this issue on Miss Owens' behalf?"

Again more silence.

In her peripheral vision, she could see Gabe looking at her, but she couldn't get herself to look directly at him. Her breath burned in her lungs, wanting to beg him to help, but if he hoped to win her heart he would have to support her without being asked.

Gabe slowly rose. "I will."

"You cannot," Reverend Colburn stated, emphatically. "You are here to learn from your father, but you aren't an elder yet."

Gabe remained standing, though he was expected to sit. His set jaw and inscrutable expression gave away neither disdain nor agreement, but he was still standing.

Mr. McIntosh shifted in the pew then stood shoulder to shoulder with his son. "I will sponsor Miss Owens' request. Olivia has given of herself in a way that no other young woman in the settlement has. My children are learning from her and look forward to their time with her all week. She is especially patient with my Barnabus, teaching him to read though he cannot hear or speak, and Rebecca and I are grateful. Miss Owens is right. Our children would benefit from daily instruction."

Reverend Colburn removed his spectacles. "All right, Thomas. We will discuss the matter of building a schoolhouse in the future, but not tonight. Thank you, Miss Owens. If that is all, we must continue our business in an orderly manner. Gabriel, would you see Miss Owens home, please?"

Gabriel left the pew, and Mr. McIntosh sat back down.

As Olivia turned to walk to the chapel door, her father put his head in his weathered hands. She hadn't meant to hurt him. Her chin dipped to her chest and she hurried for the exit.

Gabe pushed the door open and closed it behind them. She expected him to offer his arm or give her some touch of reassurance. Instead, he shoved his hands into his pockets and descended the steps in front of her.

She gathered the edge of her shawl around her neck to shield her skin from the wind that blew ahead of the storm. Gabe rushed across the lawn and toward the road. In her haste to keep up, her ankle turned on a rock. She released a wordless curse and slowed her pace. Though shadowy and cold outside, she'd rather walk by herself in the dark than be hurried.

Gabe kept walking. In all the years she'd known him, she couldn't recall ever having seen him angry. It didn't suit him.

She'd rather be alone than be treated poorly, now and in life. "If you are hurrying me home so you can return to the meeting, just go back right now. I got myself here and I can see myself home."

He forcibly exhaled. "Reverend Colburn said for me to take you home."

She stopped walking. "If you are trying to punish me, I don't deserve it and I won't have it."

He abruptly halted his steps and looked back at her. The wind blew his hair across his forehead. "You shouldn't have come here tonight."

"I did it for the children."

"You did it for yourself."

"Not so!" she yelled, unintentionally.

"You owe your father an apology."

Her heart hit the wall of her chest. "I did what I had to do because he didn't do what he should have done."

"What about me?"

"You think I owe you an apology too?"

"No. But how about a thank you?"

"I planned to thank you, but you are in such a rush to get me home, I wasn't sure you would have time for it. But now that you have stopped: thank you, Gabriel McIntosh, for standing up for me."

"A little less sarcasm would make it more palatable."

"Well, you should have spoken up for me weeks ago. You wouldn't, so I had to come here tonight and make the request myself."

He jerked his hand from his pocket and jabbed himself in the chest with his fingertips. "So now it's my fault?"

"No. It is mine." She lowered her voice. "I care about the children in this settlement and am devoting my life to teaching them. My request for them was not being heard so I did what I had to do." She stepped forward, closing the distance between them, but he still felt miles away. "I appreciate your standing up on my behalf, even if you don't understand the passion that drove me to interrupt the meeting in the first place. I am grateful to you and to your father for sponsoring my cause. Whether the schoolhouse gets approved or not remains to be seen. But you stood up for me and I'm grateful. The rest is out of my hands now... and yours."

Thunder rumbled in the distance, matching their tones. Gabe didn't move. He only looked down at her. His eyes pleaded with her, but for what she didn't know.

She would not apologize. She had already thanked him. There was nothing more to be said. She turned her face away to break his stare. "You can return to the meeting. I don't need to be chaperoned home."

"No. I said I would see you home and I will."

"I don't want to walk with you if you're angry with me." She glanced at the chapel behind them. "I expected to argue with Reverend Colburn tonight and maybe some of the elders if they became vexed, but not with you."

"I'm not angry with you, Liv. I'm frustrated by the whole situation. It shouldn't be this hard. Our settlement needs a school. I have the lumber. My father and I are carpenters. There is plenty of land. And you are right that this shouldn't be so hard. But this is the system the men agreed on before they left America and they are sticking to it. I'm sorry."

"Me too."

A roll of thunder drew his attention to the east. She expected it to reignite his urgency, but when he looked back at her, his expression had softened. He offered his arm. "I guess this is what you meant when you asked if you had my loyalty."

"Yes. And you did stand up for me tonight." She took his arm. "I don't expect anything else from you."

"That's just it... you should expect more from me. I'm going to become one of the elders here someday. I agree with most of their rules. But it wasn't fair that they ignored your request for so long. You shouldn't have had to come here tonight." He smoothed her hand over his arm. "Let me walk you home."

CHAPTER EIGHT

Mud slurped beneath Olivia's boots as she walked home from teaching at the Ashtons' house. The storm had left puddles on the rain-soaked road and thick clouds in the afternoon sky. A chill crawled over her skin, and it wasn't from the cold. She pushed her long braid over her shoulder to cover the back of her neck.

Mrs. Cotter was standing on the sandy lot across from the chapel, speaking in frantic but hushed tones with Mrs. Roberts.

Olivia nodded a greeting to the whispering ladies as she passed.

Neither reciprocated, but only scowled at her. Mrs. Cotter shielded her mouth and leaned toward Mrs. Roberts as she filled her ear. Mrs. Roberts flared her nostrils at whatever Mrs. Cotter said and shook her head in disapproval at Olivia. Their gossipy susurrations carried on the wind until Olivia made it home.

As she opened the back door, her three sisters walked out, one at a time. She held the door and lifted her chin at Alice. "Where are you all going?"

Alice tied her bonnet. "To the Fosters' farm. Mrs. Foster is going to show us how to weave burlap."

Olivia wanted to go too, but she had to memorize tomorrow's lesson plans.

Inside, her mother was wiping the stove. Her father and brother were sitting in front of empty lunch plates at the table. When her father saw her in the doorway unlacing her boots, he set his cup on his tin plate. "Come on, Walter. It's time to get back to work." He left without acknowledging her, and Walter followed him.

Richie ran to the back door. "Wait for me!" he called to their father as he jumped from the porch.

Her mother closed the door behind them and then turned to Olivia. "I do hope they let Richie help with the work this afternoon. That boy has energy to spare. Your father is so focused on training Walter to cut stone that he forgets Richie is his son too."

Olivia stared out the circular window at the figures disappearing into the barn. "How long will Father stay angry with me?"

Mary returned to the stove with her rag. "What did you expect?"

She let her vision blur as she gazed outside. "I expected the elders to say *yes, you are right, we need a schoolhouse. Thank you for bringing it to our attention. We shall start building immediately.*"

"Wrong." Mary grinned sardonically. "And what did you expect your father to do?"

"I don't know." She left the window and flopped her satchel onto the tabletop. "I guess I thought he'd see how much it meant to me and to the village. Maybe he'd apologize for ignoring the issue. I didn't expect him to be so angry he wouldn't say hello to me."

"I didn't hear you say hello to him either." Her mother tossed the rag into the rinse water with a plop. "You will never have a peaceful relationship with men if you insist on castrating them."

"I did no such thing!"

"You took away his power."

"He wasn't using it."

"That was his choice."

"He chose poorly."

Mary wiped her hands on her stained apron. "You have only been teaching for a month. You are forceful with your plans and insist things can only work if they align with your ideal circumstances. The men would have gotten around to building a schoolhouse. And they will get to the salt works Mrs. Colburn thinks we need and the gristmill Mrs. Ashton wants and the iron furnace Mrs. Roberts believes is of vital importance."

"So that's why they were whispering about me." Dejected, Olivia lowered herself into a chair at the table. "I didn't realize—"

"No, you didn't. You had your mind set on your own plans and haven't stopped to consider what other needs there might be in this settlement." Mary sat on the chair beside her. "You're young and think you have to prove yourself, but you can't do it in a month. Take time to watch what is going on around you. Listen to your elders and to the parents and to the students." Mary held up a finger to emphasize a point. "That doesn't mean you should stifle your own opinions or that you should live to please everyone else, but at least listen to them."

Her mother was right. She dropped her head into her hands. "I already felt like an intruder in most of the homes, and now I've only made it worse. It's hard enough to get the students to pay attention to their lessons. Just today, James Ashton, who used to be proficient at calculus, wouldn't sit still long enough to complete a simple review. He kept going to the window to see what his older brothers were doing with the horse Mr. Cotter gave Doctor Ashton."

"There will always be some distraction for students. You should help them by making the lessons more interesting."

She lifted her head. "How? We have limited books, only a few hours together, and hardly any materials to expand the lessons."

"I'm not sure how, to be truthful. I never had to teach in peculiar circumstances like these. You have to lure them into learning. Make the lessons relevant to their lives."

Olivia almost rolled her eyes. "Mother, everyone needs to read and write and add. Those lessons are relevant. And the other lessons are all subjects their peers would be learning back home... subjects you taught us in school ten years ago."

"Yes, but instead of simply assigning reading, writing, and arithmetic homework, equip the children to solve the problems they will encounter in daily life—not daily life doing business in America, but life as it actually is for them here. These children are growing up in the throes of homesteading and building a settlement in a remote land. Someday they might enjoy learning French and calculus, but for now they need to know how to find plants that produce dyes, how to turn flax into linen, and how to test well water."

"The parents are teaching practical skills, aren't they?"

"Some. But every family has different knowledge. Find out what your students need to learn."

"Either formal education is needed and we should establish it, including a schoolhouse, or it isn't needed and we should just spend our time quilting."

Mary tilted her head and sighed. "Try not to become bitter. We are all learning as we go. We are teaching each other."

"I know in my heart I am doing the right thing." Olivia looked toward the overcast light filtering through the front windows. "All I've ever wanted to do is teach school. I believe it is my purpose... my calling."

"And I believe that too." Her mother stood and tied on her bonnet. "But I suggest you make the lessons apply to your students' lives... especially while you are fighting to get their attention and their parents' approval."

Mary gathered her gloves and basket and left to check the crab traps at the shore. The house fell quiet, save for the crackling gray leaf log on the grate. Olivia withdrew her lesson planner from her satchel and carried it to her mother's rocking chair in the parlor. She had work to do.

She lifted the cover of the journal she'd spent two years filling with lesson plans. Her pencil markings on the first page of notes made sense. The monster was asleep or away or had died. How she had begged the Lord to please let it die! God could remove the impairment from her permanently if He chose. Thus far He had not. But in these moments of clarity, she worked as efficiently as she could. Unless the Lord removed this thorn, her ability to read written words might be momentary.

She had worked this hard through a difficulty no one knew about, except Doctor Ashton. If the other elders knew, they would respect her less. Not that she had increased their respect last night, but she'd at least won the chance to have her cause heard. Her work was not done yet. It might never be, especially if some of the other women had building projects they wanted prioritized in the settlement.

She would do everything in her power to increase respect for education in the students. She needed to capture their imaginations in one class time per week. And the lessons had to be relevant enough to settlement life to make the parents want the children to have more lessons... daily lessons... a proper school.

What could she teach the children that would interest them, benefit them, and incorporate language and arithmetic? She leaned her head back and stared at the crossbeam in the ceiling as she tried to think.

The rhythmic sway of the rocker relaxed her. She'd barely slept last night after barging into the elder meeting and now her mind wanted a break.

So many thoughts and voices swirled in her head. Gabe had asked her father for his blessing. She had broken one of the settlement's rules. Her mother said her lessons were boring and irrelevant. Mrs. Susanna Vestal was ill and no one knew but her, the doctor, and Mr. Vestal. Marian said Gabe was trustworthy and in love with her. Her father was angry with her. Women in the village were gossiping about her. She wanted to be free from the impairment that stole her ability to read. Gabe wanted more for her... more from her...

The late afternoon sun peeked out beneath the cloud line to the west. It shone through the front window, sending dust-speckled chinks of light across Olivia and the chair. The rocker was still. Her open mouth wet her sleeve. She lifted her head and glanced around the empty house.

It was late. The afternoon was almost gone. Precious working hours had been slept away without her knowledge or permission.

Her lesson planner was upside down beside her stocking-covered feet on the rag rug. She wiped the drool from her chin. As she leaned down to pick up the journal, her hair fell loose across her shoulder. She reached for the ribbon that she always kept tied around the end of her long braid. It was gone. She pulled the loose strands in front of her face. Her hair was ten inches shorter than it should be.

Her breath caught as she shot to her feet. She searched the chair, the rug, the folds in her clothing, but couldn't find any cut pieces of hair. Someone had come in the house while she napped and cut off half of her braid.

And they had taken her hair with them.

Who would be so cruel and daring and violate a person in her sleep? Had an elder attacked her femininity in retaliation for her interrupting their meeting? Had her growing relationship with Gabe driven Peggy to maddening jealousy? Had her father wanted to punish her? No, he might have been perturbed by her behavior last night, but he would never lift a hand against her. Maybe it was Mrs. Cotter. She'd been rude and hateful toward her since school started. But would Mrs.

Cotter leave her family during the day, sneak into the house, and defile a person so brazenly?

Children's voices rang outside the house.

Olivia ran up the stairs with her lesson planner in one hand and the other hand buried in her now shoulder-length hair. Once in the bedroom, she darted for the basket on the foot of Alice's side of the bed and rifled through her sister's things until she collected several hairpins.

She stepped to the washstand and swirled her hair into a knot behind her head. Her fingers shook as she pinned her hair into a chignon. Loose strands fell out to frame her face. She pinned them back too, as not to draw attention to the shorter length.

The door opened downstairs and her sisters surged in the house all talking at once. As the girls climbed the stairs and ran into the room, Olivia tucked in the last strands of her straight black hair.

"What's this?" Alice cooed as she spotted Olivia. "Trying a new hairstyle?"

"I borrowed a few of your hairpins. I hope you don't mind."

Martha gazed up at her in the mirror. "You look like a grown up lady."

"I am a grown up lady." She tried to sound unaffected, but her voice broke. "I just wanted to do something different."

Almeda snickered. "Now you look like a schoolteacher."

"I am a schoolteacher."

Alice craned her neck to see the back of Olivia's hair. "It doesn't look as bulky. Did you cut it?"

Olivia scrambled for a true but simple explanation. "My braid was damaged." She gave each of her sisters a quick look. They had no idea what had happened to her. "It's time I start arranging my hair in a more mature fashion anyhow."

The girls tossed their bonnets and shawls onto the bed and chatted about their time with Mrs. Foster. Martha held up a piece of burlap. "Look what I made."

"Very good," Olivia said as she sat beside Martha on the edge of the bed. She reached out to feel the freshly woven material, but her fingers were shaking. She rubbed her hands together. "My, it's cold in here."

Her sisters didn't know someone had been in the house and mistreated her. But someone knew. Whoever did this was capable of anything. They had cut her hair this time. What if they hurt her or one of her sisters next time? She should tell someone, but whom? If she didn't know who did it, how could she know who to trust?

Surely the perpetrator would give away his or her guilt. They would say something to someone or reveal themselves somehow. She would wait and watch for a clue.

She stepped to the window and looked out. Gabe was walking toward his family's house next door. He would notice her hair had been cut. He noticed everything about her.

CHAPTER NINE

Olivia smoothed her hair while she waited for Marian to answer the door. In a week's time, she'd grown used to her new hairstyle, but her fingers continually checked the pins. The new gesture was becoming a habit. Other than the initial *you've changed your hair* comments, no one in the settlement had seemed to give it another thought. Or at least they didn't let on if they did.

After staying home last Thursday afternoon and having someone sneak in and chop off half her hair, she couldn't bear the eerie stillness when the house was empty, especially with the heavy autumn clouds outside. She'd endured another week of wearisome house-to-house teaching, whispering women, and disapproving glances. And Gabe was still out on his property, hewing lumber for his house.

She missed him. She didn't want to miss him. It might mean something that she wasn't ready to accept.

She needed the company of a friend, and Marian needed pencils. Thus, she knocked again.

Marian opened the door with a naked baby in her arms. "Olivia, what a nice surprise! Come in," she said over her shoulder as she took the baby back to the bed where a clean diaper had been laid out.

Olivia stepped inside the warm cabin. It must be pleasant to be the lady of the house, no matter how small the home. She imagined having her own cabin. She could do whatever she wanted, whenever she wanted without dodging parental scowls and snide sibling remarks. She could keep the lamp on and read all night when the monster was away instead of squinting to see the words in the moonlight as she had last night.

No wonder she was tired. She sniffed the air. "Do I smell coffee?"

"In aroma only," Marian said with a wistful smile. "Jonah is finally letting me experiment with the coffee-scented leaves from the bush down shore, but he made me promise not to ingest it and to keep it away from the baby."

"Smart man."

"I pressed the leaves and blended their oil into our candle wax. I was hoping the smell might hide some of the diaper stench."

"It had me fooled." Olivia pulled off her gloves one finger at a time as Marian scooped the freshened baby from the mattress. She stuffed the gloves into her satchel and withdrew a string-tied bundle of a dozen graphite pencils. "I brought you something."

"Gracious!" Marian widened her eyes as she accepted the pencils with her free hand. "Are you sure you can spare so many?"

"I should think so. I brought ten gross with me from America."

"Smart woman." Marian examined the red cedar pencils. "Mr. Roberts said he knows how to hand make them—"

Olivia gave her voice a masculine affectation. "Once we locate a graphite deposit—"

Marian also mocked a baritone. "And once we perfect our paper making process."

They laughed together, and it felt good.

When their laughter died out, Marian thanked her for the pencils and placed them on the Davenport desk in the corner of the room. Olivia pointed at the desk. "Wasn't that in the captain's cabin on the *Providence*?"

Marian nodded and nestled baby Frederick into his bassinet. "Remember when we didn't know if we would ever make it to land? And here we are, two years later with a little village."

"And a lot of problems."

"Indeed." Marian frowned and motioned for Olivia to sit at a table. "Jonah told me what happened at the elder meeting last night."

"Last night?" Olivia had not been informed. Her father was barely speaking to her as his way of punishing her for the interruption of last week's meeting. He probably told Walter every detail of the elder meetings, and maybe her mother, but certainly not her or her sisters. His air of angry displeasure had simmered into a general ignoring of her presence, which wasn't too far from normal.

She lowered herself into a chair at the table. Its top was made from a round slice of a wide tree stump. She held onto the table's lacquered edge, bracing for the news. "What happened last night?"

"Apparently several women were inspired by your, um, assertiveness last week and decided to try it this week."

"Collectively?"

"No, but Jonah said it was quite the parade."

"Oh, dear." She pressed her fingertips to her temples. "Who?"

Marian sat across from her at the little table and lowered her volume even though they were alone in her tidy home with the door closed. "First, Mrs. Roberts went into the chapel saying she needed to give something to Mr. Roberts that he'd forgotten at home. Then she went on to ask the elders if they would consider building an iron furnace so her husband could make molds for the machinery that would ease his production work."

Olivia leaned back in the chair. "How did the elders react?"

"Mr. Roberts apologized for her intrusion and escorted her home before they could respond. While they were gone, my own mother gave it a try."

"What on earth for?"

Marian began to blush. "She said if Susanna Vestal was allowed to miss church on Sundays on account of being tired, she thought such reprieve should be granted to all women with small children. She said Sundays are a day of rest for men but getting a jump on the day before the service steals hours of sleep that weary mothers desperately need."

The mention of Susanna being simply *tired* made Olivia's stomach ache. That was the excuse Mr. Vestal had relayed for her the past few weeks. It was true she was tired, but it was more than fatigue. Susanna could hardly get out of bed, let alone attend church. Mr. Vestal and Doctor Ashton knew it. The village deserved to know, but Olivia couldn't say anything, even to her dearest friend. She faltered for words. "What... what do you think of your mother's request?"

"Unnecessary." Marian shrugged. "I have to get up twice each night to nurse Frederick, and I make it to church just fine. It's healthy for mothers to get out of the house and be among the community each Sunday. Mother probably thought she was being helpful by speaking up for all women."

"What did the elders tell her?"

"Jonah said she made her request, excused herself, and left before anyone could say anything. But that wasn't all. As they were about to end the meeting, Mrs. Cotter went into the chapel and clapped to get the men's attention. And you won't believe what she wanted." Marian paused to build anticipation. "She said we must stop all building projects and construct a ship so that anyone who is ready to leave this land and sail home will have a way to do so."

Perhaps that was why Mrs. Cotter behaved so strangely... she wanted to go home. It wasn't possible, and everyone in the settlement knew it and had seemed to accept it. After all, the group had intended to settle on secluded land when they left America. Regretting such a permanent relocation would be heartbreaking. Imagining it made her sorry for Mrs. Cotter. "It's simply not possible. Hasn't she heard about the currents around the shore? She saw what happened to the *Providence*."

"She said they should build a ship to be fair to those who want to leave. Apparently, she was quite forceful with Reverend Colburn. When Mr. Cotter tried to escort her out, she began arguing with him and saying we are all going to die here."

"I don't agree with her request or her poor behavior," Olivia touched her hair and wondered about Mrs. Cotter's sanity, "but I understand why she felt she should take her concern to the elders. We've been told to keep our peace over everything for so long and now some can't discern what is a valid village issue and what is not."

"It might feel that way, but that isn't entirely true."

"This is what happens when leaders exclude half of the population simply because we are female."

Marian shook her head. "Jonah said the elders didn't want to exclude women because they are female. He said they have to exclude them all because some of the men say their wives would be ridiculous in public debate over business issues."

"Mrs. Cotter's behavior probably helped prove that case, but men can be ridiculous too."

"The elders found last night's meeting to confirm their system is best for the settlement."

"And it probably hurt my cause. Shame too. This is yet another example of why we need to establish formal education. We must give the next generation the ability to use logic to voice concerns."

Marian patted her arm. "Do try to be patient with the elders. They have the settlement's best interests in mind. This will all turn out fine in the end. I know it will."

"That's why I love coming to your house. I need your encouragement. At least that's part of why I came today." A strand of short hair fell over Olivia's eyes. She flinched to brush it back, but stopped herself and pointed at the strand. "I didn't do this."

"Do what?"

"Cut my hair. When you—and everyone else—asked about it, I said my braid had been damaged. While that is technically true, it's not the whole truth." When Marian furrowed her brow, Olivia continued. "The day after I interrupted the elder meeting last week, someone came into our parlor while I was napping and cut my braid clean off. Took it with them too."

Marian's mouth fell open. "Who?"

"I don't know. I thought whoever did it would act suspiciously around me or tell someone and it would get back to me, but no one has said anything."

"Do you think it had to do with your going to the elder meeting?"

"That or a prank by a student or maybe someone was jealous that Gabe is paying attention to me—"

"Peggy?"

"I don't know. No one has given any clues or given my hair a second glance."

"It looks normal, like all the other ladies' hairstyles." Marian shrugged. "Maybe it wasn't malicious."

"An accidental hair clipping on a sleeping woman in her home?" Olivia laughed louder than she intended and covered her mouth. "You truly see the best in everyone, don't you?"

Marian chuckled. "I suppose I do." Her concerned expression returned. "The truth will come out. Have you told anyone else?"

Olivia shook her head. "I caused enough of a stir last week."

The hinges on the door squeaked as it opened. Jonah stepped into the cabin.

"Darling!" Marian met him at the door, grinning widely.

"Get the baby and go to the chapel." He barely gave her a peck on the cheek as he rushed to his medical bag, which was on the floor beside the desk. "I have to hurry to the Vestals' farm."

Marian followed his quick strides across the room. "What's wrong?"

"It's Susanna Vestal," he said as he picked up the medical bag. He whirled back for the door and looked at Olivia. "You need to go to the chapel too."

Olivia stood. "Is Mrs. Vestal all right?" she asked, knowing the answer.

Jonah paused at the door, gripping the handle of his medical bag. "She is near death. My father has been treating her condition privately for some time, but there was nothing else to be done for her. I'm going with him to the Vestals' now. Reverend Colburn said for everyone to go to the chapel to join together and pray for her. Divine healing is her only hope for remaining in this life." He pulled Marian close and kissed her before he left. "Pray."

* * *

Olivia carried an extra blanket for the baby and walked with Marian to the church. People were coming from all directions, still dressed in their work clothes. Dirty hems and muddy boots ascended the chapel's stone steps ahead of her as the worried villagers gathered to pray for Susanna Vestal.

Reverend Colburn held the arched wooden door open for everyone. His somber greeting was the same to each person as they entered. "Once everyone has arrived, I will give the details of Mrs. Vestal's condition. Go in and find two or three others to pray with."

Marian entered the chapel first and whispered over her shoulder to Olivia, "Jonah is assisting Doctor Ashton and my family isn't here yet. Stay with me."

"Of course." Olivia gave Marian's arm a reassuring touch and felt her tremble. "Are you all right?"

"Yes, this is just such a shock." Marian stayed close to her and walked toward the window on the north side of the chapel. "Aren't you shocked?"

Olivia glanced out the window. If she admitted she knew Susanna had been ill and she had kept it secret, she might seem cold-hearted. Unless she added that Doctor Ashton knew too and Mr. Vestal, and they were all abiding by Susanna's request. Then Marian might become upset with Doctor Ashton for not telling the community about it, or even Jonah if he had prior knowledge, which by the look on his face at the cabin, Olivia doubted he had.

But Marian wasn't asking them if they were shocked at the news of Susanna's conditions; she was asking Olivia.

Maybe she should have told everyone weeks ago despite Doctor Ashton's directive. They all could have been praying for Susanna this whole time. Maybe God would have intervened if they had all prayed instead of just her. Oh, how she'd prayed. Every time she walked into the Vestal home or saw the children at church or thought of Mr. Vestal being left to raise six children, including twin toddlers, alone.

"You knew, didn't you?" Marian whispered on a breath.

Olivia picked at the folds in the spare baby blanket she held and tried to think of an explanation. None came to mind. "Yes."

Marian's chin quivered. "Has she been suffering?"

"Just overcome with fatigue from what I saw, but she never appeared to be in pain."

"What is the illness?"

"I don't know."

"Cancer?"

"She was very private about what she was going through."

Marian pressed her lips together and looked at the ceiling. "Can you imagine going through something dreadful and keeping it hidden?"

Olivia stared at the binding around the edge of the blanket. The baby's name and date of birth were stitched in block letters. She could read it clearly at the moment, but the fear of word blindness haunted her daily. "Yes, I can imagine that."

"Must be pride that keeps people from asking for help when they need it."

"Pride... yes, I suppose you're right."

"We are all wretchedly prideful though, so none of us can blame one another, can we?"

Olivia traced a finger along the stitched letters. "No, we cannot."

Marian's gaze moved to someone behind Olivia. Before Olivia could turn to see who it was, she felt a hand on her shoulder.

"Miss Owens." Mrs. Roberts sniffled into a scallop-edged handkerchief. "This is a sobering reminder of the fragility of life, is it not?"

"Um, yes ma'am."

Mrs. Roberts dabbed her crying eyes. "Olivia, I fear I treated you quite rudely the other day. Would you forgive me?"

Olivia thought back to how Mrs. Roberts had been whispering with Mrs. Cotter the day after the elder meeting and had given her a mean look. It didn't seem to matter now. "Yes, of course, I forgive you."

Mrs. Roberts thanked her and walked on to Mrs. Colburn where she began another apology, but Olivia couldn't hear the details.

The chapel pews were filling up as more people arrived. Those who had been aggravated with each other hours before were now embracing and praying together. Olivia wondered if Mrs. Cotter would make any requests for forgiveness. She looked back at Marian. "I wanted to tell you about Mrs. Vestal, but I was told not to."

Marian gave a short nod. "Don't feel badly."

The light caught Marian's eye for an instant. Something caused her delight even amidst this grief. Olivia followed her line of sight. Gabe was walking toward them. He put a hand to both of their backs. "My father went to get the Fosters and my family isn't here yet. May I pray with you?" he asked as he glanced from Olivia to Marian and back.

"Please do," Marian replied. She turned in so the sleeping baby was at the center of their little huddle.

Gabe bowed his head and began to pray. "Holy Father, thank You for hearing our prayer. Thank You for being our salvation, our comforter, our provider, and our healer. You are good and we are humbly grateful. We know that all things work together for good to them that love You. We do love You, Lord. With hearts submitted to Your will, we pray You heal Mrs. Vestal. Please give her comfort and peace and remove this illness from her body. We don't want to lose a member of our community in death, and we pray You allow Mrs. Vestal more time on this earth for our benefit and for her children. But if it is Your will to end her illness through death, we know nothing can separate her from Your love, which is in Christ Jesus our Lord. You promised us Your peace, which passes all understanding. Comfort our hearts with the knowledge that to be absent from the body is to be present with the Lord. We pray for Christopher Vestal to have courage and peace in this time of agony and for the Vestal children to trust You even as they face the possibility of losing their mother. Please bind this community together with hearts that long to glorify You."

As Gabe prayed, Olivia's heart filled with peace she'd never known. It was quickly followed by a surge of sweet and pleasant affection, beyond admiration, for Gabriel McIntosh. She opened her eyes, still wet with grief, and watched him as he continued beseeching God on behalf of the Vestals and the community.

He knew the scriptures and loved his Lord. He lifted their prayer in a way she'd previously only witnessed in ministers.

His faith awakened something in her heart, something she did not know it was capable of.

It did no good to tell her eyes to close; they were fixed on this man beside her. He had his hand on her back and his heart before the Lord. How had she not noticed his faith and leadership before? What else had she missed while her heart had been hardened? Or had God waited for the right time to soften her heart toward the right man?

Gabe ended his prayer and his father motioned for him to join their family. Olivia wanted him to stay beside her. He wouldn't know that. He wouldn't know about any of the new and exquisite feelings that were crackling inside her awakening heart.

Reverend Colburn called the room's attention, and Olivia and Marian slid into the nearest pew to sit. The reverend gave what few details he had of Mrs. Vestal's condition. Having witnessed Susanna's decline first hand, Olivia knew more about the situation than the reverend. When he completed his announcement, hushed murmurs rippled across the pews as concerned conversations began throughout the chapel.

Olivia leaned close to Marian's ear. "Remember what we talked about when we were collecting seashells before the campfire last month?"

"Yes," Marian whispered.

"You asked me to tell you when I knew... how I felt."

Marian's eyes shot to hers. She mouthed, "Now?"

"Yes, while he was praying. I couldn't help it. I felt my heart might burst out of my chest with its next beat. I didn't mean for it to happen. I wasn't even thinking about such things. It is most inappropriate to fall in love now, considering the circumstances."

The edge of Marian's mouth curved faintly. "Love rarely waits for ideal circumstances."

Olivia tried to keep from continually looking at Gabe. "You once pitied me because I'd never been in love."

"I no longer pity you... only your timing."

Olivia scanned the worried villagers. Most were forming little groups and praying. The baby stirred in Marian's arms. Olivia held out the extra blanket. "Is he cold?"

Marian shook her head. "Just a restless sleeper."

"Me too."

Olivia checked the window to the north. Jonah was walking briskly down the road toward the chapel. "He's coming with news."

"Oh, thank God."

The gray overcast sky met the gray leaf trees in a cold and monochrome landscape outside. Dismal as it appeared in winter, tea made from the gray leaf tree once saved Marian's life. It gave Olivia an idea. "Do you think Jonah and Doctor Ashton would consider giving Mrs. Vestal the gray leaf tea?"

Marian shook her head rapidly. "They never were convinced the tea healed me and they believe it was the cause of my coma. They have forbidden its consumption until it is proven to have medicinal value."

"How can they prove it if they don't try it again?"

"I agree with you, but I won't suggest it to Jonah."

"Why?"

"It is important to my marriage that I respect my husband's decisions."

Jonah removed his hat as he came through the chapel doors. The church fell silent. He loosened the green scarf at his neck as he walked the side aisle to the front of the chapel and spoke privately to Reverend Colburn.

The reverend closed his eyes and blew out a breath through pursed lips. Finally, he looked out at the waiting congregation. "Mrs. Susanna Vestal has gone to be with the Lord."

CHAPTER TEN

L ong lines of white clouds puffed like lambs wool in the cold afternoon sky. Olivia ambled through the settlement toward the Vestals' property. As the road dwindled to a footpath near the meadow by the orchard, she slowed her pace even more. The ache of losing a member of the community was still as fresh as Susanna Vestal's grave. The tombstone was too far from the road to see, but it was there on the mowed earth beyond the incline.

What could she possibly say to the Vestal children on the first lesson after their mother's passing? She didn't have proper lessons planned. She'd brought a storybook to read to them if they wanted her to, and if her eyes would cooperate. She'd cut and folded little cards for them to write things about their mother, to keep for when they grew up and forgot her face. And she planned to listen to them if they wanted to talk about their loss, but she still felt ill prepared.

Christopher Vestal was raking the ground between the trees at the edge of his orchard near the house. His rake swiped the same piece of ground over and over. His yellow dog was lying in the sun behind him as if they had been there a long while.

"Good afternoon, Mr. Vestal," she said as she approached.

The dog lifted its head from the ground.

Christopher glanced up. The brim of his straw hat concealed his brow. "Hello, Miss Owens. Is it afternoon already?"

"My first lessons were canceled this morning, so I might be a bit early. Is it all right that I came today?"

Christopher leaned on his rake. "Yes, of course. The children were hoping you would come. They are all in the house, except David is in the barn. He wanted to be alone."

The dog strolled over to Olivia and began sniffing her fingertips. She opened her hand to pet its wide head. "I didn't plan on teaching today, just being with the children and helping out around the house if they need me."

"Your kindness is most appreciated." He cast his gaze toward the meadow, no doubt toward the tombstone just out of view. "It still feels frightfully lonely in the house without..." He returned his gaze to her then. "The children will be glad to have you with them for a few hours." His lips moved slightly as though he had more words to say, but hadn't decided whether or not to speak them.

She wished she had the effusion of encouragement Marian possessed or Gabe's lighthearted humor or Jonah's wealth of knowledge. No helpful words came to mind. A grieving person stood before her with something to say. She could only listen. She stepped closer and waited in the shadow of Christopher's silence.

The dog moved toward its master and leaned against his leg. Christopher looked down at the dog but didn't offer it affection. He raised his hat with a knuckle. "My mother died when I was ten—the age Wade is now. My siblings and I had to take on the housework and cooking. I remember working constantly to try to distract myself from grief, but still feeling hopelessly forlorn. We were happy when my father quickly remarried." He turned his sad eyes back to the meadow. "Susanna was sick for so long. I didn't expect her passing to be the shock that it has been to me. I thought I would feel relief for her and for myself. But the grief comes in sudden pulses. It suffocates my soul without warning. My only hope is in knowing she is with the Lord and no longer suffering. Now I wait for God to rescue my heart from this pit."

"I'm so sorry." Her heart hurt too, but not as severely as he described. She'd never experienced that kind of pain. "What can I do?"

Christopher pressed his lips together. "You are here. That is the most any person can do. The children are looking forward to your visit."

"I brought activities for them if they need a diversion. Mostly, I thought they might like some company."

"Quite right."

"Is there anything you need done around the house? Shall I bake something?"

He shook his head. "The village ladies have brought us more food than we can eat. And plenty of help too, thank the Lord. Rebecca McIntosh minded the twins this morning and said she would each Monday as long as we need her to. Hannah was grateful to have the time so she could do the washing without worrying about the little ones. And Catherine Foster will be keeping them on Thursdays."

"How gracious."

"Indeed." The light briefly hit his eyes. "Your own mother said she'd keep them on Saturdays so Hannah could rest. She said a fourteen-year-old girl shouldn't have to mind five siblings all day every day."

Olivia had often helped with her five siblings when she was that young, but never without their mother nearby. She offered a slight smile. "I look forward to seeing the twins in our home on Saturdays then."

Little Doris stepped out the back door of the house and the twins toddled behind her. The girls' voices carried across the yard to the edge of the orchard. "Miss Owens! Miss Owens!"

"And hearing them?" Christopher grinned at her. "You will certainly hear them."

"Yes, that too." She chuckled at his humor, and his kind expression warmed. A laugh amidst sadness felt like a shooting star on the blackest night. Even in his grief, Christopher Vestal was easy to talk to.

Olivia waved at the girls then looked back at him. "I should go in. Would you like to join us?"

He shook his head. "I have work to do."

"Of course," she said as she started for the house. "Do come inside if you change your mind. And let David know he is welcome to join us too."

Christopher nodded then returned to his mindless raking.

Doris ran across the yard and wrapped her arms around Olivia's waist, hugging tightly in the way children do when they don't yet know their own strength. Olivia let her cling a moment then smoothed Doris's hair. "Let's go inside. I brought a storybook."

Hannah stepped onto the stoop and pinned the last of her laundry to a line strung from the porch to a gray leaf tree in the middle of the yard. The twins peeked out from behind her. She opened the door for Olivia. "Hello, Miss Owens. Wade ran upstairs to get his reader." Though only fourteen, Hannah resembled her mother, same high cheekbones and long lashes. "I'll be putting these two down for their nap soon, so you shouldn't be disturbed while you teach."

Olivia climbed the two stairs from the mudroom into the kitchen with Doris still holding onto her waist. "Thank you, Hannah, but I wasn't planning to teach today unless the children want lessons."

One of the twins whimpered for Hannah to pick her up. She hoisted the small child to her hip and followed Olivia into the kitchen. "Whatever you think is best."

Olivia opened her satchel and pulled the storybook out. She offered it to Doris. "Take this into the parlor and pick out a story for me to read you in a few minutes, all right?"

Doris let go of her. She accepted the hardbound storybook and dashed into the parlor. One of the toddlers followed her, squealing, unaffected by the haze of tragedy in the air.

Hannah was in the corner of the mudroom. She still had the other twin on her hip and was trying to slide a laundry board into its place with her free hand.

Olivia hurried to help her. "Let me get that."

"Oh, thank you." Hannah pointed between the shelves. "No, it goes there. At least that's where mother keeps it... kept it." Her chin wrinkled and she squeezed her eyes shut. "We're almost out of soap," she slurred while holding back a sob.

Olivia glanced about the shelves. "Pardon?"

"Soap. Mother made our soap for the year every fall and she didn't this year. I never learned how. We only have enough for another few weeks."

She touched Hannah's arm. "I can teach you how to make soap. I know it's not the same as your—"

"You can?" She opened her eyes. "You would?"

"Of course. Did your mother save grease drippings?"

"Always. I still do."

"And ashes from the hearth?"

"Yes."

"Good. I'll talk to your father about soaking the ashes for lye. I'm sure he has a barrel in the barn. How about next week when I come for lessons? We will ask Mrs. McIntosh to mind the twins for the afternoon, and instead of book lessons, Doris and Wade can watch and learn how to make soap too."

"That would be helpful."

"Then it's settled."

The Vestal children needed to learn a certain practical skill and Olivia needed to prove the value of education to the settlement. If she incorporated writing the instructions and calculating the recipe into the demonstration, teaching the children to make soap might be the kind of relevant lesson the students of Good Springs needed.

Olivia held out her hands, offering to take the toddler from Hannah. "Would you like me to put the twins in bed for their nap?"

"No, no," Hannah sniffled. "They won't stay in bed unless I do it. They are used to me tending to them. Mother was sick since soon after they were born, so I've done it all."

"How can I help?"

Hannah wiped her tears with her sleeve. Her grieving face looked more mature than fourteen yet innocent with childhood all at once. "Just stay, if you don't mind, till I come back down."

"I will." Olivia glanced into the parlor, where Wade was joining Doris, awaiting their lessons. "While you put the twins down to nap, I'll get Wade and Doris started on a story. Then we can talk."

While Hannah took the youngest of the Vestal brood upstairs, Olivia flipped through the storybook with Doris and Wade. Wade wasn't interested in it and asked if he could study his reader instead. Olivia read the titles from the storybook to Doris, letting her pick a story, but she only wanted to look at the pictures.

"Keep the storybook here this week and look at it all you like, Doris. Next week our lesson will be outside."

"Outside?" Wade perked up. "We get to learn something outside?"

"That's right." Olivia smiled. "We're going to take our tablets outside and you will learn to write notes as I teach you and Hannah a very important process that you will use for the rest of your life."

Doris and Wade gazed at each other with eyes widening with curiosity.

CHAPTER ELEVEN

Olivia lingered in the chapel with the crowd long after the Sunday service had ended. Though past lunchtime, no one seemed to be in a hurry to go home. She hummed The Doxology to herself and wished it were warm enough outside for a picnic so all the church families could spend the afternoon in leisure together. Winter had not yet settled on the land, and she was already aching for spring.

The loss of Susanna Vestal had tightened the bonds of the community, and a chorus of conversations filled the high-ceilinged room. Some people were still sitting in pews; some were clustered in the aisles and near the door, hats and shawls in hand. Occasional laughter rose from one pocket of conversation or another, proving time would thin their grief.

Olivia stood with her mother at the back of the chapel as Mrs. Colburn told them about her baby's development. "He's already rolling over," the reverend's wife said, beaming at her infant son. Then she looked at Olivia's mother. "Oh, Mary, he is going to be a smart one."

A tug on Olivia's sleeve drew her attention down to little Jane Cotter, who wanted to show off the lace cuffs her big sister had made her. Olivia fawned over the pretty lace, much to Jane's delight.

At once, Doris and Wade Vestal both squeezed past the crowd to get to Olivia. Wade had his reader tucked under his elbow. Olivia was hesitantly pleased that he'd taken his schoolbook to church, though she hoped Reverend Colburn hadn't noticed. Doris greeted her with a tight hug and bounced a little as she spoke. "I'm so looking forward to our lesson tomorrow!"

"I'm glad you are."

"Hannah told us you're going to teach us how to make soap." Doris unfurled her arms from Olivia's waist but held her hand. "Will it be bubbly soap?"

"Not this kind." She smiled at Doris. "But I'll show you how to make it smell nice."

Doris glanced back when her father called her and Wade to the door. She frowned. "We have to go home now."

Christopher Vestal held one of his toddlers and Hannah had the other twin by the wrist. David stood behind them, scowling. Wade went to his father, but Doris didn't let go of Olivia's hand.

Olivia's heart sank while she watched the Vestal children assemble to go home without a mother. She knelt to be eye level with little Doris. "Thank you for coming to see me. I will be at your house after lunch tomorrow, and we will have such fun making soap."

Doris gave a sad nod and left with her family.

Olivia felt her own mother's watching eyes. When she rose, Mary inclined her head. "I'm proud of you."

"What for?"

"The children are quite fond of you, and it sounds like you are figuring out what they need."

Olivia wanted to say that what the Vestal children needed was their mother back, but Reverend Colburn's sermon still rang in her ears. She shrugged. "They are in God's hands. We all are."

"And we all need each other." Mary patted her arm and turned to greet Mrs. Cotter.

Already dreading tomorrow's visit to the Cotters' house, Olivia didn't want to spend any more time around Mrs. Cotter than she had to. Still, she was curious as to what the woman might say.

Olivia glanced around the room, pretending not to listen. Her siblings were scattered throughout the chapel, chatting with other youngsters, and her father stood a few feet away, discussing stonework for an oven of some sort with Mr. McIntosh. Gabe was at the front of the church speaking with two of the elders.

Mrs. Cotter prattled on about cooking. Her chipper tone was a stark contrast to the one she used in her home, at least whenever Olivia was there. Mary listened attentively as Mrs. Cotter detailed her family's love of her custard recipe. The more Mrs. Cotter boasted about making cheese and whipping cream, Olivia wondered how much her mother would listen to before her suspicions were raised.

Finally, when Mrs. Cotter mentioned churning a barrel of butter, Mary's brow contracted and she spoke up. "I'm surprised you can spare so much milk with one cow and a family of nine. Our cow doesn't give milk half the time."

Mrs. Cotter's spine straightened, and her eyes moved rapidly from side to side.

Mary continued. "When it was just the cow, I thought maybe someone's calf was getting loose and drinking from her, but now one of my hens is missing too…"

Mrs. Cotter raised a finger as if an idea had suddenly come to mind. "It sounds as though someone is stealing from you." She lowered her voice. "And I suspect that someone is Benjamin Foster. Remember, Benjamin stole the guns when we were on the ship and threw them overboard. And Benjamin did start the fire that destroyed the chapel's wood. He is a mischievous young man and might be stealing food now too. Wouldn't surprise me in the least."

Mary held up a hand, halting the gossipy speculation. "Now, let's not accuse anyone."

"Benjamin Foster is a troublemaker." Mrs. Cotter's voice cracked. "If anyone else mentions milk or hens or anything being stolen, I will expose that boy for the thief he is."

"No need for that." Mary dropped her hand and took a step back. "Let's forget I mentioned the milk."

"I'll be keeping an eye on that boy."

"Enjoy your custard today, Cora. Good day."

"Good day to you, Mary." Mrs. Cotter poked her nose into the air and crossed the room to Peggy and her other daughters.

Olivia watched Mary's face and waited for her mother to make eye contact, hoping to give her a look. Mary only leaned in and whispered, "Let's hope no one else has a dry cow or a missing hen or that woman will do her best to ruin Benjamin."

It wasn't fair for Benjamin Foster to always get the blame when something was amiss in the settlement, especially when there was no reason to believe he stole anything. He'd kept to himself since the incident with the fire two months ago.

Olivia wished she could tell her mother that a thief had been milking the Vestals' cow too, but she couldn't spread news from one house to the next. She held back a frustrated sigh. "Do you find it interesting that the person with excess food is the person casting blame?"

"Interesting, but not conclusive."

"Does Mrs. Cotter seem different to you since we settled here?"

Mary sent her a sidelong glance then started picking invisible lint from her dress sleeves. "It happens to women sometimes. Probably a hysterical condition. Maybe her womb is tipped."

"That is no excuse for her to—"

Mary bristled. "Not in church, please."

Mrs. Cotter and Peggy stood on the other side of the room, whispering and looking at Gabe. He had his back to them, speaking with Jonah and Henry. Whatever he said stirred a raucous laugh from the men. Olivia wanted to join them.

He glanced back and met her gaze. He watched her for one long moment then excused himself from his conversation. When he passed the Cotters, Peggy brushed her hand along his arm and said something with a coy smile. Her dainty lace cuffs swallowed her limp wrist. Olivia imagined leaping across the pews and choking Peggy Cotter with the delicate trim. Instead, she kept her focus on the man she was falling in love with.

Gabe ignored Peggy's advance and kept walking along the outer aisle of the chapel toward the back where Olivia stood by her mother. Half of her wanted him to scoop her into his arms in front of everyone and half of her wanted to avert her eyes so he might leave her alone in the crowd. That was the half that used to win, but the new feelings that stirred inside her were beginning to overpower her insecurities. She rarely had occasion to speak with him now that it mattered, and her anticipation grew with each step he took closer.

He paused near her father then held up a finger to her and mouthed *don't leave*.

She nodded and watched expectantly for his next move.

Her mother leaned in close. "Your father told me about their conversation."

"Hm?"

"Gabriel has your father's blessing. It's about time you—"

"Shh, not now Mother," Olivia spat as Gabe and her father came over.

Richard put an arm around Mary, jauntily. "I've invited Gabriel to our house for supper."

"That's a very fine idea," Mary said with delight spreading across her face.

Richard wrapped his callused fingers around Mary's shoulder. "But first he is going to take Olivia to see his house…. what is built of it so far anyhow."

"Oh, how lovely." Mary smiled at her.

Gabe put his hand to Olivia's back. "That is, if you would like to."

"Of course she wants to see the house you're building!" Richard's unusual display of excitement drew attention from those nearby. "Take your time, Gabriel. Take your time and show her the house and the property. You want to go, don't you, Livy?"

Her cheeks felt like they had been splattered with molten lava. She wanted to disappear into a puff of smoke and seep between the floorboards unnoticed. "Yes, of course."

She managed an inelegant goodbye to her overjoyed parents and walked out of the chapel with Gabe. The cold winter air took the heat out of her face. She waited until she was at the bottom of the stone steps to look at him. He slapped his hat onto his head and buttoned his overcoat. The crisply ironed collar of his shirt paralleled the strong line of his jaw.

The chapel door closed, muffling the voices of the crowd inside. Gabe scrunched his nose and grinned sheepishly. "I had no idea your father would become so… elated. I'm sorry that was awkward for you."

"Oh, don't be," she said as she slipped on her gloves. "I'm growing accustomed to embarrassing moments in the chapel."

He chuckled at her joke. "At least your parents seemed pleased."

"True." She thought for a moment. "Actually, that was the first time my father has smiled at me since I interrupted the elder meeting. So I'm grateful for his jubilant reaction."

Gabe widened his eyes. "I'm grateful they approve of me."

"Me too."

He grinned at her but didn't say anything.

She lifted a gloved hand. "What?"

"That might be the highest compliment you have ever given me." He flipped up the collar of his overcoat. "Are you simply glad they approve of me or do you approve of me as well?"

She faked an aristocratic tone and raised an eyebrow at him. "How terribly forward of you, sir."

He laughed at her affectation. "And you are terrible at pretending to be pretentious."

"That might be the highest compliment you have ever given me." She echoed his words then smiled up at him. "And yes, I approve of you."

He took her hand as they crossed the chapel yard. As their laughter died out, she glanced back at the chapel. Peggy was standing near the window, watching them.

Gabe glanced back too. He squeezed her hand. "Don't worry about her... or her mother... or any of it. Just look forward."

She tried to look forward, but her eyes insisted on studying his profile. He'd pursued her for months, maybe longer and she hadn't realized it—or hadn't allowed herself to because of Peggy's lies. Now the desire she felt for him roiled inside her like clouds before a storm. To think it all began the day she heard him pray.

Being near him filled her with an intoxicating mixture of delight and devastation. It distracted her mind from everything else, and he didn't even know. He mattered more to her now than anyone. His opinion of her meant more than anyone else's. If she lost his admiration, she might never recover. "Just look forward," she repeated on a breath.

He'd taken her hand so easily. She wished she wasn't wearing gloves so she could feel the warmth of his skin. After only a moment connected to him, she felt weightless. Her worries, the cold wind, the problems in the settlement, the monster that haunted her teaching and threatened her profession, it all settled into the recesses of her mind like a foggy memory or a forgotten dream.

Her skirt swished as she walked with him westward on the path toward the big stream. Even under an overcast sky and with the deciduous trees dormant, the land held beauty in its majestic and mysterious grip. A fawn grazed beside its mother on a grassy slope in the distance. Birds fluttered from the silvery canopy of the gray leaf trees and glided to the tips of nearby figs trees. It would be pleasant to live near the stream, but it seemed odd for an outgoing man like Gabe to build a home away from the others. "Why did you choose to live out here by yourself?"

"I'm not by myself. Mr. Weathermon's cabin is nearby. He was by himself."

She scanned the path ahead but didn't see any structures. "What does he do alone all day?"

"Fishes mostly. He gathered wild blackberries until the first frost. Brought me a bucket of them once."

"Mr. Weathermon? I didn't know he liked anyone but the Ashtons."

"He likes me because I built his cabin." He winked at her. "All he wanted was a quiet place to retire and fish. His heart condition doesn't allow him to do much."

"That seems lonely."

Gabe shrugged. "Jonah checks on him every day. And since the main structure of my house is complete and I'm working alone, he often walks over in the afternoons."

The surly former shipping tycoon rarely said a kind word to anyone but the Ashtons during their voyage on his ship two years ago. Now he rarely went into the village. She imagined Gabe going out of his way to relate to Mr. Weathermon. "It's generous of you to accommodate him."

"He's pleasant company, has a fine sense of humor," Gabe chuckled, "and he's finally come to faith in Christ."

"I'm pleased to hear it."

"You'll like him once you get to know him." He glanced behind them. "And we aren't that far away from the village. I enjoy being out here. The fishing is good in the stream and there is plenty of space."

"It would be lovely to live close to the stream, especially one so wide and cold. When I was a child, I'd go swimming every summer in the river near my grandparents' farm."

"I know."

She glanced at him. "Oh, did I tell you that already... that I enjoy swimming?"

"No, not directly." He slowed their pace. "One summer back in Accomack, we were all swimming at the Andersons' place. Remember them?" When she nodded, he continued. "You were about fifteen and were there with Peggy and Marian and the Anderson girls—"

The summer memory from her teen years flooded back. "I do remember that! The cool water felt refreshing. Mrs. Anderson had made us girls each a set of swimming clothes— dark blue tops and matching pantaloons. The older boys would hardly leave us alone. They kept going under the water and catching our feet just to hear us scream." She laughed. "I didn't go swimming very often after that. But I sometimes think of how good the cold water felt."

"It was hot that day."

"Odd, I don't remember you there." She faked a scowl. "You weren't one of the boys catching our feet under the water, were you?"

"No."

"Throwing frogs?"

"No."

"Staring when we'd climb the bank wet?"

"Probably." He held up a hand in surrender. "I was sixteen. You made quite an impression on me that day."

"I'll bet." She laughed.

He chuckled too. "Not because of the wet pantaloons."

"Why then?"

He fixed his gaze ahead of them. "You were a totally different person out there on the bank of the river than you were in class. It was like you'd shed your seriousness and whatever that great burden was you carried around. You dropped your bonnet and the sun gleamed off your dark hair. When you jumped feet first off the bank, you took my heart with you. I knew then the only way to get my heart back was to win yours."

She felt her mouth drop open but closed it before he looked at her.

"When I was building Mr. Weathermon's cabin, I would stare out at the stream and imagine you there, swimming and laughing, free and happy in the sun and water." He squeezed her hand. "You asked why I chose to live out here... that is why."

When they reached the end of Jonah's property, Gabe lifted their joined hands and pointed. "This is my land from here to those trees to the creek at the edge of the Cotters' farm and all the way back to the big stream."

The grassy path had been worn to dry stubble, and it widened as they approached the clearing. Woodchips and sawdust covered the earth. As they passed a stack of gray leaf logs and cut stone, she looked up at the house.

"What do you think?" he asked, smiling nervously.

In style, the house matched the other log structures in the settlement, but this was higher with two full stories. Wide openings gaped where windows and doors were needed, and a timber frame outlined where the stone chimney would be built.

She stopped, still holding his hand. "It's beautiful and... bigger than I expected. I guess I had pictured it more like the cabins in the village."

He chuckled once. "I learned from all the additions we had to build on those cabins. I wanted to build my home to suit a family from the beginning."

"A family?" she said aloud without meaning to.

"Of course. Remember, I built by the stream with you in mind." He gave her hand a gentle tug. "Come on, I want you to see inside."

The sharp minty scent of freshly hewn gray leaf lumber filled the air. He guided her through the jumble of sawhorses and splintered wood to the open doorway at the back of the house. Then he stepped up onto a tree stump that served as a stair to the threshold. She raised the front of her skirt to follow his steps, but he clasped her waist and hoisted her inside.

Her hands reflexively dropped her skirt and gripped his shoulders. As her feet touched the floorboards, she watched his face. He kept his fingertips on her waist for a moment longer than was necessary. His lips curved in a satisfied grin. Then he let go as quickly as he'd scooped her up.

He pointed at the ceiling as if nothing had happened. "It took six men and a system of pulleys to get the logs onto the roof. Each log weighs over three hundred and fifty pounds. Mr. Roberts came up with that number somehow."

"Did he?" she responded, still breathless from the surprise of him lifting her.

"He's a smart man. Good with figures and all of that."

"Apparently."

"Henry takes after him."

"Yes."

Gabe didn't look at her, but she could tell he was smiling. "The upstairs will have full ceiling height instead of a cramped space like the lofts in the village cabins. You can see the stream from the dormer windows upstairs. I would show you, but I haven't built the staircase yet. The men helped raise the structure, but the interior building is up to me. I like it that way. My father and brothers will help when they can. Jonah too. But otherwise, I'll work on it alone all winter."

"I see." Her eyes trailed up the rope ladder. She imagined climbing it clumsily and was glad he hadn't suggested it. She looked back at Gabe.

He pointed at the southern wall. "And your father and Walter are going to start building the stone fireplace and oven this week."

"Excellent."

He put his hand to the small of her back. "What do you really think?"

She couldn't think. Her thoughts congealed into a mush of foreign urges and blocked all hope of logical conversation. At last, she found her voice. "Of the house?"

He looked at her lips and his grin disappeared. She watched the blue of his irises as he studied her. He didn't move but somehow felt closer. Too close.

She put her hand to his chest and turned her face away. She scanned the wide unfinished space looking for something, anything to comment on. "I think your house is, um… it's the start of something beautiful."

He covered her hand with his. "Something is different."

"With the house? I wouldn't know because—"

"No, something is different about you… about us."

"Us?"

"Yes, us."

Us? Were they a couple? Courting? It was all happening so fast and everything inside her wanted it to keep going, but she didn't know what to do or say. She had never been in a relationship with a man, and though she'd heard plenty of caution to women about prudence, she certainly didn't want to put out his fire… not again… not when hers was freshly ablaze. She swallowed her hesitation. "Are we an… us?"

"I hope so. I have been planning to marry you since we were staying at the Ashtons' estate in Accomack County, preparing for the voyage."

"I didn't know… not like that…"

"I'm in love with you, Liv. I have been since that day at the river in Virginia five years ago." His eyes implored her. "Now you know. But I don't know if you feel the same way about me. I think you might, but you confuse me at every turn. I know something has changed in you. I can see it when you look at me and I can feel it in the way you breathe when I touch you. But I have waited so long for this and I won't allow myself to believe it until I hear it from you."

She opened her mouth, but no words would come out. Yes, she was in love with him, but how could she say it and so soon? He deserved to know how she felt, but once she told him, her heart would be in his hands. Then he would want to know her more. He would want to know everything about her. She wasn't ready for that. "I don't know what to do."

He dropped his cheek to her forehead. "Just say something. That's all I want for now—to finally know you feel the same for me."

With her face buried against his collar, she whispered. "I'm afraid."

"Are you afraid that if you say you are in love with me, I will have you at the reverend's door within the hour?"

She pulled back to see him smiling. "It crossed my mind."

"I won't. Not until I know you are ready. Not until I'm certain I have won your heart."

Her gaze moved down his face to his mouth. Whisker stubble shadowed his chin and darkened the lines where he was always grinning. If she couldn't tell him how she felt, perhaps she could show him. Her eyelids fluttered shut and she lifted her lips toward his.

He drew his face back before she could kiss him. "Don't."

Her heels dropped to the floor. "What's wrong?"

"Don't do that."

"Do what?"

"Forget your worth."

One thousand questions flooded her thoughts. She shook her head. "I don't understand."

"Liv, your worth is far above rubies."

"Far above rubies?"

"You are a virtuous woman and a precious treasure to me. I want to kiss you, but that isn't why I brought you here."

"I'm sorry." Her heart pounded in her throat. She hadn't meant anything lascivious by trying to kiss him and she certainly wasn't going to offer more. If it wasn't bad enough that she didn't know what to say, now she was doing the wrong thing. She looked down at her feet. "I told you I don't know what to do."

"You don't have to because I do. Your father trusts me with you. I need you to let me lead." He gently raised her chin.

"I have thought about this for years. I'm not looking for a sweetheart; I want more than that. I want a life with you. I won't rush you to the altar, but you have to let me lead. Can you do that?"

After pursuing her for so long, he wasn't ready to end the chase. That only made her want to try and kiss him again, but if his way of acknowledging her worth was to lead her in courtship, she would let him. Gladly. She shut her mouth and managed a rigid nod.

He stood still, gazing down at her. Only his crystalline eyes moved as he studied her. Each beat of her heart ticked the seconds as she waited for his lead.

A grin curved the corners of his mouth. "Good." He took her fingertips in his hand. "We'd better go back to the village before rumors begin."

CHAPTER TWELVE

Olivia hummed as she walked to the Vestals' farm, carrying a pail full of tallow. She had spent Sunday evening humming through the stinky process of rendering the fat for the Vestals' soap. Twice this morning she had caught herself humming during the Cotter children's lessons. Even Mrs. Cotter's strident behavior couldn't dampen the joy of being in love.

As she walked to the Vestals' property, the cold wind and overcast sky were no match for the warmth in her heart. Gabe loved her. He was not the insincere flirt she had once believed him to be, but rather a caring gentleman who had pined for her for years. Being near him brought her dead heart to life and almost made her forget the ugly secret she'd have to confess if they became as close as she hoped they would.

Three of the six Vestal children were waiting on the path between the orchard and the meadow. Hannah and Doris waved vigorously when they saw her coming. Wade was playing tug-of-war with the dog, but once he noticed her, he waved too.

Seeing their excitement to learn and even just to spend time with her laced her joy with appreciation. Students like the

Vestal children made her want to be a teacher the rest of her life despite the difficulties she might face.

"Good afternoon," she greeted.

Wade ran to her and took the covered pail from her hand. "What is in this?"

"Three pounds of fat."

Doris furled her thin but strong arms around Olivia's waist and walked awkwardly beside her to the house. "Father has the wood ready for your fire—"

"And he said I could light it!" Wade interrupted.

Hannah scowled at her little brother then she tucked a strand of light brown hair behind her ear and smiled sweetly at Olivia. "Before Father left today he set out all the things that were on your list." She counted the items off with her fingers. "The old pot, two jugs, a measuring cup, a stirring stick, work gloves, and wooden spoons."

"Excellent." Olivia had hoped Christopher Vestal would be around when she taught the children the necessary but potentially dangerous process of soap making. She also wanted him to be there because he was nice to talk to. His fatherly presence made her feel like everything would be all right, even though he was the one who'd recently endured tragedy. She gave the orchard a quick scan. "Where did your father go?"

"Fishing," Doris answered quickly. "He took David to the stream. Said they will come back with our dinner. I love fried fish."

"As do I," Olivia grinned at the girl then looked over at Hannah. "What about the lye?"

"He left the pan below the ash hopper."

"Then we can get started right away," Olivia said as she and the children approached the yard at the side of the house. Everything she'd asked for was set out on a board near the perfectly arranged firewood. "I wanted to explain the lye process to you before we begin."

Doris let go of her and picked up a slate and chalk. "I'm ready to make notes like you said, Miss Owens."

Wade held out the pail of fat. "Where do you want this?"

"Get the fire going and we will melt it in the pot."

Doris scrunched her nose. "Is that lard?

"No, fat obtained from pigs is lard. When it's from cattle, sheep, or deer it's called tallow."

Doris made marks on her slate, guessing how to spell tallow. Then she crinkled her smooth brow. "Why don't we have any pigs here?"

Olivia thought back. "Mr. Roberts was the only farmer in our group who had pigs back in Virginia. He had his drove slaughtered for salt pork for the voyage. And there aren't any wild pigs here—none that we've encountered yet anyway."

Hannah selected a wooden spoon from the tools and helped scoop the fat into the pot. "It was miserable eating salt pork every day for three months on the ship."

"Salt pork sounds good to me," Wade said as he stoked the fire.

Hannah shook her head. "No one old enough to remember the voyage would want to eat pork again."

While the fat melted in a pot over the fire, Olivia followed the children into the barn. They proudly pointed out the ash hopper, though they didn't know how it worked. Olivia explained, "Your father filled the bottom of this wooden box with ashes then covered the ashes with a layer of straw. He probably poured a little water here frequently over the past few days. The water seeps slowly through the ashes and the liquid lye drips down this trough and into this pan. Does anyone know how to figure how much lye you will need?"

The children glanced at each other. Hannah pulled a folded piece of paper and a stub of pencil out of her apron pocket. She turned and folded the paper until she found a blank spot and waited for the formula. Their expectant enthusiasm to learn a necessary skill confirmed Olivia was doing the right thing. This was the sort of lesson the children of Good Springs needed, and often.

She held up the measuring cup to the scant light coming through the barn doors. "All of the ingredients, including your water, must be measured accurately. Since we have about three pounds of rendered fat, we will need four cups water and ten ounces of lye. This was my grandmother's recipe and it will make about ninety ounces of soft soap. That isn't a year's worth for a family your size, but I want you to have to make it every few months for a while so you will remember the process."

Hannah slipped on her work gloves and carried the jug of measured lye back to the house. Her arms were stiffly bent away from her body. "What happens if it gets on my skin?"

"Vinegar will neutralize the burn," Olivia answered, realizing she hadn't asked Christopher to leave vinegar close at hand. If she wanted to be in charge of a schoolhouse full of children someday, surely she could take care of three students by herself. She remembered the fire on the first day of school and doubt filled her thoughts. "Please, be cautious with it. Keep your gloves on and your sleeves down."

While the fat melted in the pot over the fire, she let Hannah measure the water into a glass jug. "Always add the lye to the water. Never the other way around or you will cause an eruption." She slowly stirred the lye into the water. "As this mixes it will warm. We will let it cool then add it to the melted fat and stir it as it boils."

The children diligently watched all afternoon. Hannah made notes at each step of the process. Doris wrote a word or two on her slate. Wade got jittery with excitement at the end of the boiling when the mixture rose into a frothy mass. Olivia decided he would be the first to learn how to taste the mixture to be sure it was done.

"No way," he balked when she demonstrated placing a small cooled amount on the tongue to see if the bite was gone.

"You must learn."

"Oh all right." He reached a finger to the spoon and winced until his tongue touched the drip of soap. Then he grinned. "Not bad."

Doris wrinkled her nose. "Do I have to taste it too?"

"Not this time," Olivia answered. "But you will have to learn eventually."

After she gave instructions on letting the soap cool and showed them how to store it, they began to clean the utensils. A brief part in the clouds allowed a stream of sunlight to break through the late afternoon sky. It was time to end her lesson. "I helped my grandmother with soap making every year when I was a girl. After she died, my mother bought our soap from the general store, but I always missed the annual chore with Granny." All at once she realized none of the children in the settlement of Good Springs had their grandparents in their lives any longer, though many were probably still alive back in America. She almost asked the Vestal children about their grandparents, but since they had recently lost their mother, it might refresh their sadness.

The dog sprang from its place beside Wade and rushed to the path. Mr. Vestal and David were returning with their catch hanging from lines over Christopher's shoulder. When they reached the house, Christopher passed the fish to David and brushed his hands together as he met Olivia by the back steps.

She held up the cleaned jugs. "Do these go in the mudroom?"

"Here, I can take them in." Christopher pushed up the brim of his straw hat. "You have done so much for us today."

"It has been a pleasure."

"How did they get along?"

"Quite well. Very attentive and helpful." She stopped, still holding the jugs. "We will do this again in a few months, but I will oversee the process instead of instructing next time."

He reached for the glass jugs. "Are you able to stay for dinner?"

She glanced at the children. They seemed happy, settled by a full day's work and occupied with the fish David began to clean. She had nowhere urgent to be. Her mother wouldn't expect her home early and she probably wouldn't see Gabe again until church on Sunday. "Sure. I can help cook if you need me."

A grin deepened the creases at the outer corners of Christopher's eyes. "I didn't mean for you to stay and work. One of my only kitchen skills is frying a fresh catch. Consider it our way of saying thank you."

"Sounds delightful."

As Christopher opened the door to go into the house, Olivia gathered more utensils. She bent down and picked up the measuring cup and spoons. When she turned back to go inside, Christopher still stood on the stoop, holding the door open for her.

They returned the utensils to their place in the mudroom then he hung his woolen coat on a peg by the door. "The children enjoyed your company today. I could tell by their faces from across the yard. They are very fond of you."

"And I them." Unable to stand idly while he cooked, she crossed the room to the stove and checked the gray leaf chips burning in the firebox.

"Have a seat at the table. You have earned it." He waved her back as he continued talking. "When the elders first discussed building a schoolhouse, I barely gave it a thought. But you have convinced me with your passion." He cuffed his sleeves and began washing his hands in the basin. "I've never known a woman to have such fervor for something that she keeps at it despite resistance." He lifted a wide iron pan from its hook on the wall beside the stove and began to season it. "I'd heard of women behaving boldly for this cause or that back in America, but it usually left me with a bad impression. You went above protest by showing us how much you care about educating the children."

"Thank you, Mr. Vestal."

"Christopher, please."

She reluctantly lowered herself into a chair at the table. "Thank you, Christopher."

"I like having you come to the house to teach the children. It is convenient for me to have them here all week. But you have proven you know what you're doing, and you have the courage to stick with it. I've decided to champion your cause of getting that schoolhouse built soon. I can't promise the elders will agree with me right away, but I promise to show the same determination in persuading them that you have shown in teaching my children."

Olivia shot to her feet. "Thank you, Mr. Vestal, I mean Christopher! That means a great deal to me."

He gave her a quick grin over his shoulder as he held his palm over the stove, checking its heat. "You are important to my children, so if having a schoolhouse is important to you, it is important to me."

CHAPTER THIRTEEN

A rosy film of morning light settled across a thin layer of fresh snow. Olivia's boots crunched through the white ice as she walked between the gray leaf trees on her family's property and turned right onto the road toward the Roberts' cabin.

She surveyed the McIntoshes' home as she passed. Over a month had gone by since Gabe first took her to the house he was building near the stream. Even though he had told her he would be staying there to work until it was finished, she wanted him to come back to the village more often.

Diamonds of yellow light ignited across the smooth blanket of snow between the road and the McIntosh house, but it didn't distract her from hoping to catch a glimpse of Gabe. He wouldn't be there. He would be working diligently on his house, snow or no snow, because he was trying to finish it for them, for her. Still, she didn't look away from his family's house until after she passed.

She had thought she would get more attention from him once they were a couple, not less, but he was busy building a house and working hard for their future. And she was happily occupied with teaching, so it shouldn't matter. But it did now that she was in love. Her heart ached with feelings she didn't know what to do with.

The dusting of snow covered the forest floor, outlining once hidden nests and burrows. A jackrabbit peered at her through the sprigs of a bare branch. She stopped to watch him. At night the sounds along the roadside made her skin prickle, but the quiet of the bright morning after a snowfall made her believe nothing truly bad could ever happen in this land.

Or maybe being in love lightened her heart to everything, save her own imperfections.

Gabe loved her now, but would he always? Her secret involved a strange and inexplicable affliction. Who could see clearly but become suddenly blinded to the written word? No one but her, that's who. As a child, she had been the only student who could read one moment and not the next, and she learned to hide it well, even from the teacher—her own mother. No one else in class had to study as hard as her or had to memorize passages through the night.

As an adult, it was natural to channel that same determination into her profession, but marriage would expose the truth. A man wouldn't want her for a wife if he knew she was faulty. A man would be humiliated to have such an odd wife, and surely he would be repulsed at the thought of her impairment being passed to their children. She no longer feared he would laugh at her, but even with his good humor, Gabriel McIntosh would not be able to joke this flaw away if he knew.

That was it then: he could never know. If she could hide it from her mother, maybe she could hide it from a husband.

A husband. That wasn't something she ever thought she would have to consider. He hadn't proposed yet, but he had asked her father's blessing and said he wanted her for a wife. He just didn't know the whole of what he was asking for.

The rabbit's long ears twitched, but the rest of it went perfectly still. At once, it looked directly at her and then turned and bound away, as if it had heard her thoughts and didn't want her defective eyes watching it another moment.

A voice came from behind her on the road. "Miss Owens," Reverend Colburn called out as he hurried toward her. "Are you on your way to the Roberts' house?"

"Yes, sir."

The reverend came beside her, slightly out of breath. He shoved his hands into the pockets of his overcoat. "I have business with Mr. Roberts this morning. Mind if I speak with you on the way?"

The reverend had gone from the gentle pastor her family often invited to dinner back home in Virginia to the settlement leader who spent months opposing her one request. What could he possibly want to speak with her about alone on a cold morning? "I don't mind," she answered smartly before her bewilderment took her voice.

His breath made quick white clouds on the morning air as if he'd been running to catch up to her. "Thank you and good morning."

"Good morning to you too, Reverend."

As they walked along the snow-covered road, she glanced back over her shoulder. Smoke rose in grayish brown ribbons from the scattering of chimneys in the village behind her. Two figures in the distance caught her eye, both of them girls about the age of Editha and Eveline Cotter. They each had a pail in hand and were hurrying away from the Ashtons' shed. What were they doing there so early on a cold morning, and did they have the Ashtons' permission?

The reverend looked back too. "Is something the matter?"

She gave him a sidelong glimpse, wondering if she should mention her suspicions of the Cotters. She decided against it. "It's a lovely morning, is it not?"

"Indeed. Miss Owens, I have heard about the lessons you have been teaching lately." His nostrils flared, and she braced for a lecture. "It is the same report, but comes to me from different parents and even some of your students."

"Oh?"

"Seems your adding practical instruction to the lessons has changed a few opinions of your teaching. It shows wisdom on your part to make your lessons relate to the children's lives as they are now, not as they would have been if they were growing up in America. I might have underestimated the importance of corporate education in the settlement."

She held back a delighted squeal and a disrespectful *I told you so* and stared straight ahead. "I'm pleased you approve of my lessons."

The reverend's voice lost its austere glaze. "I'm not sure how much you know about my wife's family history, but her ancestors once built a fine brick home and a salt works by the sea in Accomack County. Benedict Arnold burned their home, and her great-grandfather went on to become a captain in the Revolution. Did she ever tell you that story?"

"No, sir."

"It was one of the first things she told me when we were courting. Her father told me the same story days later. It gave their family a great sense of patriotic pride. Her grandfather and father rebuilt their home and continued the business of making salt from seawater. She has been using their process here, but on a much smaller scale." He removed his spectacles and wiped them on his shirtsleeve as he continued. "Our second son has shown interest in the chore lately, and even though he is but eight, he says he will one day have a salt works here like his grandfathers had in Virginia. It got my wife thinking about the work of future generations here. She now believes someone in your position could introduce children to a great many skills."

"I see," Olivia said, relaxing in the reverend's company. "Would you and Mrs. Colburn like me to start teaching your children?"

"No. Not the basic subjects, anyhow. She enjoys teaching them at home. She would like the children to get to participate in some of the practical lessons, like the ones you have been teaching lately. If you would allow them to."

"I'm sure it could be arranged."

"And she wondered if other children in the village might like to learn about salt making. If you thought they would, you could organize the class and she would demonstrate the process for them as a group."

"What an interesting proposal." She swallowed her desire to point out she had wanted to teach the children as a group all along. It was called *school.* She nodded agreeably instead. "The children would enjoy learning together. Would I plan for such classes to be held at your home?"

"We haven't decided yet." He settled the eyeglasses back on and wrapped their golden wire ends behind his ears. "Like I said, I have heard good reports about your new lessons. I wanted to speak with you directly about your methods before I consider any more suggestions. What prompted these new practical lessons?"

As the Roberts' house came into view, she slowed her pace. She couldn't let a private conversation with the reverend about education end without mentioning the one thing the settlement still needed. "After Mrs. Vestal passed away, I realized I needed to start integrating the children's lives into their lessons. It has sparked their attention to learn other things. There are a variety of trades represented in our group, but all of the skills have not yet been taught to the next generation. Mrs. Vestal died with her pottery wheel in their barn, untouched since we arrived. I don't know if anyone else here knows how to make pottery."

"Perhaps you could find out. And maybe we should introduce the children to more trades by having others teach too."

"Yes." Excitement bubbled inside her. "And we could bring in some of the older children, who might not have considered a profession yet. Perhaps they could train for a skill that might otherwise be forgotten."

"Yes, just not firstborn sons since they will learn their father's profession."

"Of course."

"And not every day."

"Certainly not."

Reverend Colburn grinned. "God has given you zeal for teaching children, hasn't He?"

"He has."

They stopped walking when they reached the Roberts' property. She glanced up at him and saw him not as the overseer of the settlement whose opinion dictated her life, but as a pastor who cared for the people. "Reverend, the village needs a schoolhouse. It would certainly make these group demonstrations easier on the families… and on me."

The Roberts children spilled onto their porch and called excitedly to Olivia. She gave a quick wave.

Reverend Colburn looked over her head at the children. "Continue what you have been doing, for now at least. I will discuss these matters with the elders."

CHAPTER FOURTEEN

A week passed without another mention of school from Reverend Colburn, and then another. Olivia waited up for her father after the elder meeting each Wednesday night, hoping he would tell her if the subject of education had been discussed, but he said nothing. Last night, as she'd sat at the table preparing lessons by lamplight, he'd come in at a quarter to midnight and barely grunted *goodnight* to her as he trudged up the stairs.

She hoped to catch him this morning before breakfast and before his early chores and press him for information. She lit a second oil lamp in the kitchen when footsteps scuffed the floor behind her parents' closed bedroom door. It had to be her father. He was always up first.

Boiling water rumbled in a pot on the stove, and she checked the eggs inside it. Almost done. They would cool in time for breakfast, but not before her father came out. She wanted to have something fresh to offer him to slow his morning routine long enough for her to ask if Reverend Colburn had mentioned their conversation to the elders.

Richard wrangled his suspenders over his shoulders as he stepped into the kitchen. "You're up early."

"Good morning, Father."

"You beat the sun today."

"Had a lot on my mind."

Richard plunked a kettle on the stovetop and drew a tin mug from the shelf. "I take it you heard about last night."

"From whom? You were the last person I saw before I went to bed and the first person I'm seeing this morning. What did I not hear about?"

"The new schoolhouse."

"Schoolhouse?"

"The elders agreed to build it for the settlement."

Olivia dropped the pot's lid onto the stove with a clank. "It will be built? Finally? This is wonderful news! Why didn't you tell me last night?" She waved a hand, dismissing her own question. "Was it Reverend Colburn's suggestion?"

Richard gave a tired chuckle at Olivia's enthusiasm. "No, no. It was Christopher Vestal who convinced the last reluctant elders it should be a priority. He kept bringing it up until everyone agreed."

"Mr. Vestal? How kind of him." She wrapped a folded towel around the pot handle and carried it to the back door to drain the water. "Where will it be built?"

"On the sandy lot across from the chapel—"

"Just as I'd hoped! When will they build it?"

"Mr. McIntosh said we should be able to raise the structure walls in a couple of weeks, but since he is already committed to expanding the stable on the Fosters' farm, he can't finish it for a while."

"Oh," Olivia said on a breath, wondering what another undefined *while* meant.

"But Gabriel volunteered to finish it. His brother and a couple of the Ashton boys are going to help him."

"Has Gabe even finished his house yet?"

Richard glanced at the front window. "I'll let him tell you that himself. He will be here any minute."

"Here?" She smoothed her hair. "Why so early?"

"He wanted to plan the school building with you before you went to teach today." Richard pointed to the kettle. "Make me a cup when that's ready, would you?"

"Of course." When he reached for the knob of the back door, she said, "Father, wait."

He turned back and raised an eyebrow. "What is it?"

"I didn't mean to hurt you when I interrupted the elder meeting that night. I did what I felt I had to do, but I never meant to disappoint you."

Richard nodded once and squeezed her hand gently. "Nor I you."

A light knock rattled the window in the front door, and her father waved Gabe inside. The atmosphere changed when he stepped into the house, not in any nameable way. His presence made her forget her sleeping family, her plans for the day, when she took her last breath. If they married and these feelings remained, they would never get anything done.

Richard kept his voice quiet as he spoke to Gabe. "She knows about the schoolhouse. I'm going to the barn. The rest of the house is still sleeping. Stay for breakfast if you like."

Gabe removed his brown felt hat and threaded the brim between his fingers. "Thank you, sir."

As soon as the back door closed behind her father, Olivia hurried across the room to Gabe. Gleeful, she wanted to toss her hands around his neck and celebrate the elders' decision in his arms. But after the reaction she received the first time she initiated affection, she kept her hands to herself. A smile tugged at the corners of her mouth. "Can you believe it? They finally agreed."

Gabe opened his arms, hat in one hand, and embraced her. The scents of soap and gray leaf lumber mixed with his masculine air. "I wish I could have seen your face when you heard the news."

"I doubt it has changed much. Father only told me a moment ago." She pulled away first. "He said you were coming to speak with me about the building plans."

"That's part of the reason for my visit." He grinned down at her, awaiting her response to his baited statement. At least his desire for her hadn't lessened during their time apart.

She almost asked what he meant just to continue the intrigue, but at the moment she was more excited about the schoolhouse, though only by the faintest degree. "I have never planned a building's design before," she said as she led him to the table. "I'm not sure what help I could be."

He slid a chair out from the table for her. "Something tells me you have every detail of the schoolhouse pictured and have for a very long time."

"True. But the way I have pictured it over the years has changed."

He drew a pocket-sized notepad from the lining of his coat and sat beside her. "What are some of the things that haven't changed?"

She cast her gaze to the ceiling. "A long room with windows on both sides for light and fresh air... four tidy rows of single desks... my desk and a long blackboard at the front of the room..." She kept the next part of the vision to herself: the score of adoring students and the look on their faces when she fumbled over her reading and they realized she was a fraud. She shook her head, trying to erase the image. "And bookshelves on either side of the blackboard."

Gabe's pencil scratched the notepad as he sketched a floor plan. Then he made quick marks beside each line of wall. "Something like this?"

"I'm sure whatever you build will be lovely."

He pointed his pencil to the little marks. "What about these dimensions? Do you think that will be the right size for a schoolhouse?"

The marks were a mixture of numbers and letters. A short burst of dizziness passed behind her eyes. It left as quickly as it came, but she still couldn't make sense of the marks. "Sure. Looks fine to me."

"Really? Because I am only kidding. There is no way we could build it that big."

She tried to read the marks again and envisioned a dark monster holding its hand over her eyes, just as she had imagined it her whole life. Even Doctor Ashton had told her it was not some unseen evil force that disrupted her ability to read, but some physiological malfunction they just didn't have a name for. It was time she stopped the childish picture of an imaginary monster, but how? She pressed her fingertips to her temples. "Lord, help me."

Gabe widened his eyes. "That bad of a joke, huh?"

"Oh, not because of you." She chuckled at her poor timing. "I was thinking about something else."

"What?"

"Nothing."

"It was definitely something. You looked like you saw a… I don't know… a monster."

"A what?" She flinched and regretted it.

He grinned a little. "You can tell me."

No, she couldn't. Not about that. "I'm sorry. I didn't get much sleep last night." She forced a sweet smile and pointed to his notebook. "So how big would the building need to be?"

He watched her for one long moment and she waited for him to press her again. Finally, he returned his attention to the page. He erased his marks and scribbled. "How about this? It will be about the size of our schoolhouse in Virginia."

"Yes, much better."

He started a new sketch. "And eventually, you can have twenty single desks, but if you want to open the school this year, I suggest we do something like this…" He moved his hand to reveal a drawing of a long narrow table and bench. "Seat four children at each table, and line them up like this," he said as he filled in the floor plan with drawings of tables and benches.

As she watched him sketch, she wondered if any of her students would be interested in learning carpentry. "Do you think I could gather the children one day to watch you build one of the desks? You could explain the building process, sort of like a demonstration in carpentry?"

"Sure. Why not?" he answered casually. Then he winked. "I'll try to behave myself in front of your class." He went back to sketching. "With all the men helping on the structure, we should be ready to raise it in a couple of weeks. Jonah has been clearing some of their land for pasture, and he said we could have the wood. Can you wait a few weeks for the carpentry demonstration?"

"A few weeks..." She touched his hand to stop his drawing. "I never thought about how long this will take you."

"I will work as fast as I can, but you will have to be patient."

"No, I meant this will be a great deal of work for you, and you haven't finished your own house yet."

"The house is almost done. The fireplace and oven are finished thanks to your father and Walter, and the doors are on. The windows are shuttered, but there isn't any glass left from the supplies we brought from America. We will have to do the same with the schoolhouse windows until we make more glass. But it's almost ready." He set down his pencil and took her hand in his. Thick calluses lined his skin. "I know you're happy about getting a schoolhouse, and that makes me happy to build it."

"How very sweet."

He shrugged. "This is important to you, so it's important to me."

Mr. Vestal had said the same thing to her when he committed to championing her cause. Apparently, he had done just as he said he would. She tried to imagine it. "I wish I could have been there last night when Mr. Vestal convinced the elders to allow this."

Gabe slid his hand away. "Yes, well, you've made quite an impression on Christopher Vestal. He sang your praises every time someone mentioned anything related to school. Says his children enjoy learning from you and that *you open your mouth in wisdom and the teaching of kindness is on your tongue.*"

Olivia ignored Mr. Vestal's use of scripture in describing her. She didn't deserve to be compared to the woman portrayed in the Thirty-first Chapter of Proverbs. "When Mr. Vestal said he would recommend my school to the elders, I didn't know it would be accompanied by such flattering words."

Gabe crossed his arms over his chest. "Does he stay indoors while you teach his children?"

"No. Why?"

"He seemed to know a lot about your teaching methods and manner. It sounded like he was right there with you while you give his children lessons."

"So?"

"I would think a man busy with an orchard and livestock wouldn't give up a day each week to listen to school lessons."

"He doesn't. He works very hard for his family."

Gabe took her hand with both of his. "Just as I will work very hard for mine."

"Of course." She searched his face, wondering where this strange mood had come from. Was he jealous that Mr. Vestal was able to convince the elders to build the schoolhouse when he hadn't been able to? Maybe it had nothing to do with Mr. Vestal. Maybe the new project was too much to add to his full workload. She pointed at the notebook on the table. "Are you certain you want to work on the school before you finish your house? I have waited this long, and I can wait longer."

A quick grin replaced his solemn expression. "The house can wait."

"You deserve to finish it before you start another project."

He leaned close and kept his voice quiet. "Something tells me I would never have a peaceful nights' sleep if I didn't build what you want first. Besides, I'm not just building that house for myself."

She returned his cool grin. They weren't talking about construction any longer. Her words formed on a mindless breath. "For us?"

"Yes… us." He lowered his lips to hers and kissed her so gently she first wondered if he'd touched her at all. Maybe she'd imagined it.

He paused with his mouth a whisper from hers. He had mint on his breath and a tremble in his fingers. As she inhaled the air he was finished with, he kissed her again. His lips pressed firmly against hers, leaving no doubt this time.

Her heartbeat rang in her ears as she fought the urges that rose within her. When his hand cradled her neck, she traced his jaw with her fingertips. Their lips mingled in warmth and want and the awe of a first that would only happen once in a lifetime.

This must be the passion so scorned in sermons, but so necessary in bonding two people. She would gladly accept a lifetime of it. A slight moan escaped her throat and Gabe pulled away.

His gaze flicked from her eyes to her mouth. "I had no idea you would be so… affectionate."

She touched her lips, astounded. "Nor did I."

Footsteps creaked across the floor upstairs. Olivia immediately moved away from him. He picked up his pencil and tapped it against the table, still watching her, as her siblings came down for breakfast.

CHAPTER FIFTEEN

Olivia unwrapped her lunch as she descended the Cotters' porch and walked the path from their house to the road. Faint echoes of pounding hammers floated from the village on the cold air. The structure for the schoolhouse would soon be raised and this going house to house business would be over.

As she walked out of the wooded area at the edge of the Cotter property, movement caught her eye. Christopher Vestal was meandering along the roadside nearby, picking up sticks as he went. He tipped the brim of his straw hat politely when he saw her.

She shielded her eyes from the mid-day sun. "Good afternoon, Mr. Vestal."

He met her where the path from the Cotter house intersected the road. His arm cradled a bundle of sticks. "I was just heading home from the village and thought I'd gather some twigs on my way. After our voyage, I swore I'd never pass up a good piece of kindling again."

"Very prudent indeed."

"And it keeps the road cleared for pretty young schoolteachers who are forced to walk it daily."

She smiled at him. "Not for much longer, thanks to your recommendation to the elders."

"Think nothing of it." He raised his chin at the Cotter house behind her. "How was your morning?"

"It was, um…" She vocalized a pause to stall while she thought of a graceful response. She couldn't tell the whole truth: her days at the Cotter house were always frustrating at best. Mr. Cotter kept Judah and Conrad working outside instead of letting them have school lessons, Peggy slept the morning away, Frances, Editha, and Eveline worked noisily in the kitchen, and if Olivia looked at them for even a moment, Mrs. Cotter scolded her for not minding her own business. What could be so private about baking? The awkward morning was now over, and as soon as the schoolhouse was complete, she wouldn't have to step into their home ever again. She shrugged as she pinched off a bite of her sandwich. "Same as usual, I guess."

Christopher tilted his head. "Weeds?"

"Pardon?"

"There will always be weeds in our fields… problems in our work, no matter the profession."

"There are also blossoms."

He chuckled softly and joy lit his eyes. "Then tell me about the blossoms."

"Well, little Jane is a delightful pupil. She is the silver lining of my Monday mornings." She stepped onto the road, ready to move on, but gave the Cotter house one last glance over her shoulder. Peggy and Mrs. Cotter were standing at the window, watching her and Mr. Vestal. She suddenly felt caught in wrongdoing but didn't know why.

Mr. Vestal tipped his hat toward the Cotter house in greeting, also having noticed the ladies at the window. Then he switched his kindling to the other arm and started down the road beside Olivia. "Doris is beside herself with excitement today."

"Oh? What for?"

"To see you, of course. It warms my heart after what my children have been through… are going through." He pressed his lips together. "Doris especially is longing for the schoolhouse to be completed... maybe as much as you are. She is aching to have lessons every day. It's all she talks about."

Once near the Vestal house, Doris ran past the orchard to meet them. Olivia finished her sandwich, but still had a cookie wrapped in her satchel. She gave it to the little girl.

Doris hummed as she chewed, crumbs clinging to her lips. "Mm, tastes like heaven. It's been so long since I've had a cookie. Want a bite, Father?"

Christopher shook his head. "Finish it out here before the twins see you and want one of their own."

Olivia hadn't thought of the other children when she had given Doris the cookie. She glanced at Christopher. "Sorry."

He put his hand to her back. "Don't be. You made her favorite day of the week even happier."

Doris stuffed the last of the cookie into her mouth. "I wish we had milk."

"Mind your manners, Kitten," Christopher said.

Doris swallowed her food then took Olivia's hand as they walked into the house. "Our cow didn't have any milk again today."

"I know what that's like."

"Father says we will have milk tomorrow if we make the dog sleep outside. We will, won't we?"

Olivia raised an eyebrow at Christopher, awaiting his response to Doris.

He shucked off his boots and left them in the mudroom. As he stepped up the two creaky stairs into the kitchen, he said to Doris, "Go and get your lesson books ready. Miss Owens will be right in." After Doris ran into the parlor, Christopher gazed at Olivia solemnly. "For a while I thought maybe a calf was getting to our milk cow at night, but now I know who is at fault."

"Whose calf it is getting to your cow, you mean?" Olivia asked, knowing what he meant but needing him to confirm it before she could say any more.

"No. The person or persons stealing our milk." He stepped closer and kept his voice down. "I don't want to accuse anyone, but I think I know what is going on."

"Can you say?"

"I shouldn't." He looked down at his socks. "Have you noticed anything odd while you're teaching? At someone's house?"

"Someone? Who?"

"A family with an abundance of milk, perhaps?"

If he wanted her to name the Cotters first, she wouldn't do it. Sure, she suspected Mrs. Cotter was coercing her children—probably the older girls—to steal, but she shouldn't say it. "I was told long ago not to mention my observations from one house to the next." She lowered her satchel onto a kitchen chair and began to dig for her pencils. "I wanted to tell everyone about your late wife's condition, but I didn't. I must give other families the same respect."

Christopher wiped both hands over his face. "You're right. Forgive me. And thank you for keeping our situation private. It was Susanna's request. She believed she would get better and she didn't want to be thought of as the woman who had been sick. She said we could trust you. At least she was right about that."

The mention of Susanna's final weeks of life brought a lump into Olivia's throat. She struggled to focus on the Vestals' current predicament and cleared her voice. "If someone is stealing from you, and you have a strong suspicion of who it is, maybe I could help you."

He held up a palm. "No, I was out of line to ask you. Don't tell me something you shouldn't."

"I don't mean to tell you anything." After a quick glance into the parlor, she stepped toward him. "What if we could catch the thief or thieves in the act?"

"How do you mean?"

"When someone was stealing milk from us, I wanted to stay by the window at night and watch to see who it was, but I didn't think my word alone would do much good, especially when everyone was upset that I had interrupted an elder meeting. I suspect they stole a hen from us too. And now we have milk again, but you don't. If you and I witness the theft together, the thief or thieves would know they had been caught. And if they didn't confess and stop, we would have the testimony of two before the elders."

He angled his head. "This is about more than milk, isn't it?"

"I believe a young man's future is at stake."

"How so?"

"My mother and I recently mentioned our disappearing food to a certain woman while at church. That woman said she believes Benjamin Foster is the thief and if anyone else mentions something missing, she is going to accuse him before the elders." She reached a hand to Christopher's arm to emphasize her concern. "Benjamin is not the thief. I believe that with all my heart. He has been accused of so much since we left America, and it tears him down a little more each time."

Christopher wagged a finger. "And Benjamin Foster did not set fire to the lumber by the church that morning either."

"Wait... what?"

He raised his shoulders. "It was too early in the morning to start a fire with a magnifying glass. He never told his father what happened, but I agree with you, Benjamin has taken more than his share of the blame."

"And I believe that certain woman will accuse him of this too."

He was quiet for a moment and picked at his cuticles. "Do you think one of the Cotters is the thief?"

"I should not say."

"I don't believe Teddy Cotter knows what is going on. He's a good man. And Judah Cotter wouldn't steal, but I don't have the same confidence in Frances, Editha, or Eveline."

Hearing him voice her suspicions gave her a sense of comradeship. It felt exciting and wrong all at once. Christopher was an elder and her students' father. Though she liked him and he was kind to her, he was not her peer. She withdrew her hand from his arm and motioned with it as she spoke. "It could be anyone. We are all capable of sin, Mr. Vestal."

"Call me Christopher, please. And yes, you're right. I should keep my speculations to myself. It's easy to talk to you, but I've said too much." He stepped back down into the mudroom and reached for his boots. "I like your idea. We shall watch outside tonight and, if we see the thieves, confront them and let them know this must end."

"We?"

"Yes, wasn't that your suggestion?"

"I suppose, but I hadn't really thought it through. What about your children?"

His eyes shifted and then he grinned. "How are you with mending?"

"Pardon?"

"Hannah has been putting off our mending, but if she had someone to sit and do it with, she might enjoy it more. Maybe you could stay for dinner and help her with the sewing after the younger children are in bed. I would compensate you for your time. How about apples for the rest of your life? As soon as the trees mature, of course. What do you say?"

"I will help with the mending, but it's not necessary to pay me."

"Please allow me. You have done so much for me and my children."

"And you more than repaid me by getting the elders to approve the schoolhouse." She opened her satchel and took out her lesson plan and books. "But if you insist."

"I do." He smiled. "I'll send David to tell your mother you will be helping us this evening so they don't worry."

"Very well," she replied as she carried her books into the parlor and began Doris and Wade's lessons.

* * *

That evening after dinner, Doris stayed close to Olivia, wanting to help clear the table and wash dishes. While Hannah got the twins ready for bed, David and Wade disappeared upstairs, and Mr. Vestal checked the livestock in the barn. Moments later, he returned with his yellow dog.

Hannah carried a bundle of clothes that needed mending into the kitchen. She plopped them onto the tabletop. "Doris, it's time for bed."

"But I want to stay up and learn to mend from Miss Owens."

Hannah began sorting the mending pile. "You already know how."

"I need practice."

"I'll remember that next time you rip a seam. Olivia is just going to help me get caught up." She pointed at the stairs. "Change into your nightshirt and lie still in bed so the twins will go to sleep."

Doris frowned, the threat of a pout surfacing then receding before she could be scolded. "Goodnight, Miss Owens." She gave Olivia a tight hug then went to her father.

He kissed Doris on the forehead. "Goodnight, Kitten. Say your prayers."

"I will." She yawned and traipsed bleary-eyed up the stairs.

Christopher closed the curtains over the front windows. He stepped down to the mudroom and tacked a tea towel over the window by the back door. Once the windows were covered, he sat in an armchair by the fireplace. He opened his Bible and splayed it in the palm of his hand while the dog rested at his feet.

Hannah fetched an extra lamp from the parlor. She placed it on the table near Olivia, and they sat together in the warm kitchen, mending clothes. After a long silence, Hannah's needle briefly stilled. "May I ask you something?"

"Of course."

Her young voice was barely above a whisper. "Do you like to read stories?"

"Very much." She glanced up but continued sewing as not to stifle Hannah's comfort. "Do you like to read?"

Hannah kept her eyes on the fabric in her hands. "I do. We don't have many books though—not the kind I want anyway. I like adventures and love stories. We only have the children's storybooks, which I memorized long ago."

"Me too," she interrupted without meaning to. "I have a few books you might like to borrow."

"That would be lovely. I don't often get time to read. When it is quiet in the house, I'd rather..." Hannah's gaze flicked across the room toward her father. She lowered her chin. "I rather write my own stories."

"I didn't know you were a writer. That's wonderful."

The straight line of Hannah's lips curved faintly, the spark of youth momentarily visible beneath her fatigue. "Well, it's really just one long story that I have so far... or maybe it should be several shorter stories. I'm not sure exactly. It's not finished. I mean, I thought it was finished and wrote *The End*, but now I don't feel like it's complete. I don't think I'll ever know unless someone else reads it, but..." Her lips straightened again. "Oh, never mind."

Olivia waited a beat, hoping the offer would come, but it didn't. "Would you like me to read it sometime?"

"Maybe." Hannah looked up. Her long lashes seemed darker in the lamplight. "Maybe you could tell me if there are parts that need more work and help me with my grammar and such."

"I could."

"So long as you wouldn't tell anyone. I don't want people to know I write stories. They might think me foolish. It's a foolish pursuit, really. Isn't it?"

"Not at all. Jesus told stories. We all learn from stories." Olivia pointed at her satchel. "If people didn't take the time to write stories, it would be difficult for me to entice children to learn to read, wouldn't it?"

Hannah nodded then focused again on her sewing. After a moment she mumbled, "I never thought of it like that."

The house fell silent, save for the occasional crackle of the log on the fire and the clip of scissors on thread. Olivia waited for Hannah to talk more, but she didn't. Not for shyness, but natural reserve and relief to finally have peace at the end of the day. The quiet togetherness suited Olivia too. She could easily imagine being lifelong friends with Hannah.

The dog raised its head, and its ears moved as if it heard something outside. Olivia and Christopher exchanged a brief look, but he resumed his Bible reading, and she returned her eyes to the frayed seam in a shirt she assumed was his.

As the evening slipped into night, the pile of clothes to be mended dwindled, and Hannah yawned more frequently. Olivia studied her tired young face in the light of the lamp's globe. "I can finish that last shirt. You should go to bed."

"Are you sure?"

Olivia nodded. "You put in longer days than any other fourteen-year-old in the settlement." She pointed at the perfectly sewn hem of a toddler-size dress. "And you're an excellent seamstress."

Christopher nestled a slip of paper into his Bible and closed it. "Goodnight, Hannah. I will walk Miss Owens home shortly. Keep the children upstairs, should they wake."

After Hannah climbed the steps, Christopher paced to the mudroom door and peeled the tea towel away from the window. Moonlight poured across his face and deepened the lines at the outer corners of his eyes. The dog lifted its head and watched its master.

Once the upstairs door closed, Christopher quietly said, "I'm glad she asked you to read her story."

"Me too. Have you read it?"

He shook his head. "She used to read it to her mother when no one else was in the room. I'd overhear parts, but I never mentioned it. Hannah's very private, and it was something special they shared."

Olivia finished sewing and folded the last shirt. As she set it aside, Christopher pointed at the lamps on the table. "Do you mind putting those out, please? I don't want the thief to know we're still up."

Olivia complied and the only light left inside the house came from the gray leaf log burning slowly in the fireplace. She lifted her shawl from the back of the kitchen chair and wrapped it around her shoulders.

At once, the dog sprang up and scampered to the back door, whimpering.

She asked, "Does he hear someone?"

Christopher stood by the back window peering out. "No, he thinks you are leaving."

She walked to the edge of the mudroom and sat on the top step. "How long should we wait?"

A faint smile reached Christopher's eyes. "You haven't tuckered out already, have you?"

"No, just curious."

He un-tacked the tea towel, and moonlight filled the mudroom. He sat on the step beside her. "I don't think it will be much longer." The dog flopped down between them, and he petted it. "Are you having a miserable time tonight?"

"Not at all. I enjoy being with your family."

"And this?" he asked, pointing at the window.

"I have never done anything like this before. It's quite like spying, isn't it?"

"Indeed."

"Have you?"

"No, I've never spied. Unless you call watching children from the other room spying." He inclined his head. "Does this make you nervous?"

"A bit."

"Me too, but I'm rather enjoying it. Peculiar isn't it?"

"Why?"

"I'm a father of six and an elder on our village council, yet I'm titillated by spying out my own window with the hope of confronting a milk thief."

She chuckled quietly. "You deserve some happiness."

"That's too generous. I'm a widower. I'm not sure it's proper that I find pleasure in anything just yet. When Susanna died, I thought I would never cease to mourn." He looked at her then with eyes intense in the moonlight. "I feel alive when you are around. Younger somehow. You bring joy to my life, and I thought there never would be joy again. My children laugh and smile when you're here. They adore you. I admire you and could easily find myself in love with you."

A stiff knot tightened inside her stomach. "Mr. Vestal, I don't know what to say."

"Say you will consider marrying me."

She wrapped her arms under the corners of her shawl. "I'm in love with Gabriel."

"Oh," he said while his eyebrows rose a degree. "I didn't know. I have never seen you two together."

"We are… courting, I guess. It's new to me. I'm not sure what to call it. And no, we don't get much time together, but this is the first time I've ever been in love. And—"

"Please consider me." His low voice took on a raw inflection, making him sound his age. "I need you. We need you."

"I will help you and the children all I can, and the other ladies in the village will help too. I know it's hard right now, but Hannah is managing the twins well, and Doris and Wade are learning to take care of themselves more."

When he let out a long breath, she wanted to touch him to give comfort but feared the gesture might be misconstrued. She kept her hands beneath her shawl. "You don't need me as much as you think you do."

"If it's the age difference, I don't mind. My late wife was younger than me—only thirty-four and you are in your twenties. Surely that isn't so great a difference."

"Your eldest daughter is fourteen, and I am twenty. I'm closer to her age than Susanna's. You are my father's age. You've become like a father to me. Only, it's easier for me to talk to you than my father, especially lately. I have come to admire you very much."

He pinched the bridge of his nose and sat there silently for one painful moment. Finally, he released it. "So you see me as a father-figure? Your own father ignored your request, and I took it upon myself. Is that where your admiration for me arose?"

Alas, her hand couldn't be stilled any longer. She reached over the dog and pressed her palm to Christopher's back. "No, it was your kindness that drew me. When no one else listened, you did. You asked about my days and showed you cared. I admire you greatly, but I am in love with Gabe. I never thought I had the capability and here I am truly sickeningly in love with him."

He grinned faintly at her. "Well, if it makes you sick then it must be love."

She patted his back and removed her hand. "I'm sorry, Mr. Vestal, but I cannot replace your wife."

He pressed his lips together and nodded. "I understand... and I wish you the best. You deserve to be loved well. You are kind and wise and your children will one day rise up to call you blessed." While she absorbed his gracious words, he held up a finger. "But if Gabriel breaks your heart, I will break his neck."

She couldn't imagine the kind Mr. Vestal turning violent no matter the provocation, but his sentiment was flattering. She offered a smile. "Let's hope it doesn't come to that."

At once, the dog growled and leapt down the steps toward the back door. Olivia and Christopher stood simultaneously and looked out the window. A lone figure stalked through the moonlit yard toward the barn, carrying a milk pail. A dark cloak hid the person's body shape, but they didn't move like a grown man. It was an adolescent boy or a woman, but Olivia couldn't see the face. Maybe it was one of the Cotter children. Judah was only eleven. It could be him. Or maybe it was Frances. The person seemed too tall to be Editha or Eveline, and the younger girls probably wouldn't go out alone at night.

The person looked toward the house.

Olivia sucked in a breath and stepped away from the window. "Mrs. Cotter?"

"Cora? Of everyone I suspected, I most hoped she was not the thief."

"But it is her. Look!"

"Yes, it is." Christopher sighed with frustration. "I expected to see the older Cotter girls or some combination thereof."

"Me too."

"I was looking forward to letting the dog out to frighten them and telling them they must stop stealing."

Her mouth was still agape as she watched Mrs. Cotter, who was now trying to shake open the barn door. Olivia's delight in waiting to confront the thief was smothered by disappointment. "We cannot let the dog out to scare Mrs. Cotter."

"No, we cannot."

"But she must be stopped."

He raked his fingers through his hair. "Teddy Cotter and I have been friends since I first moved to Accomack. Susanna was a maid at their wedding. She hated the way Cora's attitude changed after we came to this land, but she would never have suspected this."

"Why has Mrs. Cotter changed so much since the voyage?"

His shoulders slumped. "I don't know."

"Should we tell the reverend about this?"

"Not yet. I need to think this over and pray about it. We mustn't cause division. Don't mention any of this to anyone for now."

"All right." She wrapped her shawl tighter. "Mrs. Cotter must be stopped, but I don't want to humiliate her."

"Nor I." He leaned his shoulder against the wall as they watched Mrs. Cotter struggle with the locked barn door. She finally gave up on the milk and marched to the chicken coop beside the barn.

CHAPTER SIXTEEN

Two rows of students sat on the sawdust-covered ground beside the unfinished schoolhouse. They watched as Gabe built a long narrow table that would serve as one of the desks for the classroom. Olivia stood behind the children, occasionally pacing from one end of their semi-circle to the other.

She hadn't expected all of her students to attend the demonstration. It pleased her that a few of the parents had sent children who didn't participate in school lessons, although the presence of the three older Cotter girls made her uneasy. Did they know their mother was a thief? Had they participated in her crimes, other than using and enjoying the stolen milk? Was that why they behaved so badly when she was at their house?

In the three weeks since she and Christopher had witnessed Mrs. Cotter trying to break into his barn, he hadn't mentioned the incident to Olivia. Nor did he wait by the road for her when she went to his house for lessons, but what man wouldn't behave differently after being rejected? Now when she went to teach the Vestal children, Christopher would wave from some far off point. She'd wave back and wish he would talk to her like he used to.

Today he had sent Doris and Wade to learn about furniture building, and David had come too. Even the Colburns had sent most of their brood.

The children sat close together and watched Gabe with eager delight. At different points in his demonstration, Gabe had the students pass around a wedge, then a chisel, then a mallet. All tools the children had seen before but were not usually encouraged to inspect.

Before he attached the finished tabletop to the skirt, Gabe moved the unattached top as if the table were talking to the children. Laughter rang into the cold air. His easy humor kept their attention and warmed Olivia's heart. When he asked who would like to help drive in the final pins to join the wood, all of the older girls raised their hands.

He scanned the students as if contemplating his selection for his final volunteer and sent Olivia a rueful smile. "Maybe Miss Owens would be willing to come and show us what she has learned today."

The students looked at her, and some of the older girls giggled.

"I'm happy to." She skirted the children and tried to keep her affection for Gabe concealed while in front of them.

He smirked and handed her his mallet.

With a few stern taps, she drove the pins into holes he'd cut before class began. The pins slipped easily into place due to his expert carpentry rather than her hammering, but she returned his playful smirk anyway. Handing him back the mallet, she thanked him for the demonstration and asked the students to show their appreciation with applause.

Long after she dismissed the students, the last interested child left the schoolhouse yard. Gabe turned the narrow table upright and stepped to one end. He raised his chin at the other end of the table. "Grab that, Liv."

She started to lift it. "It's heavy."

"I wouldn't ask you if I didn't think you could do it."

She stiffened her arms and helped carry the long desk into the schoolhouse. After setting it in the empty room, she proudly wiped her hands on her skirt. "I can't believe all this was built in a month."

"Why is it so hard to believe? We built it the same way we built the cabins and the chapel. The gray leaf wood makes building easier, and all the men helped raise the structure."

"I know," she said as she perambulated the classroom. "It seems like more effort went into getting it approved than built."

When he didn't respond, she realized what she had said. "Oh, I didn't mean it like that." Her hands fluttered as she tried to shoo away her careless words. A strand of hair fell over her eye. "You have worked so hard—are working so hard. I do appreciate all that you're doing for me, for the children. I didn't mean to sound ungrateful."

With a grin, he casually crossed the floor and met her in the center of the empty schoolhouse. He brushed his hands together then traced her hairline with his fingertip, moving the loose strands off her face. "It suits you."

She inhaled his scent and briefly lost focus. "What, um, suits me?"

"Wearing your hair up like a schoolteacher. I missed your long braid when you first cut it, but now I see why you did. The students' parents are probably more apt to treat you like an adult this way."

Her fingers immediately reached for her nape. "I didn't realize you had noticed."

"I notice everything about you."

"Of course you do." She almost told him that she hadn't cut it—that someone had snuck into her home and cut her hair while she'd napped and she never found out who did it. But she'd already given him enough to worry about. And he was right in that a schoolteacher would be expected to have a more mature hairstyle, but she missed her long braid too. "I'm glad you like it."

She glanced around the schoolhouse. "I thought the Ashton boys were going to help you finish the interior work."

"I sent them home for the day." He snapped his fingers as if something had suddenly come to him. "I almost forgot it… wait here for a minute."

"All right," she said to his back as he dashed outside. She went to the doorway and held onto the frame as she leaned outside, wondering what he was doing. The briny wind blew in from the ocean and stirred the sawdust around the building. She drew the edges of her shawl closer to her neck.

Gabe was digging through a leather satchel on the ground by his tools. Finally, he stood and held up an octavo book. "I have something for you." His comfortable grin stirred her as he brought it to her.

"What is this?" she asked as he stepped back into the shelter of the schoolhouse. She opened the book's clothbound cover and read aloud. "*The Courtship of Miles Standish and Other Poems* by Henry Wadsworth Longfellow. I didn't know you read for pleasure, especially poetry and romanticism."

"This is one of my favorites." He leaned his palm onto the wall beside her. His thick shoulder hovered over her. "Have you read it?"

She had borrowed a copy of the book from a friend in Virginia, but had been blinded to its words and had given it back before the voyage. She shrugged. "Some of it."

"Would you like to read it again?"

"Very much."

"Then it's yours."

She gave the dog-eared pages a quick flip. The few books brought to this land were priceless treasures. "I will borrow it, but I couldn't possibly keep it, especially since it's your favorite."

"I insist. You take far better care of your books than I do mine. And they will all end up in the same home one day soon, I hope."

She pressed the book to her chest and covered it with both hands. "Thank you."

The book yearned to be read, so she opened it. As she prepared to read the first line aloud, the letters dissolved into an unknowable mass of marks on the page. She closed her mouth and waited for the misery to pass. Alas, it did not.

"Well?" Gabe asked, waiting.

If she married him, he would discover her secret eventually. She couldn't hide her shortcomings from someone who was so close his breath entwined with hers. "Well what?"

"I thought you were going to read it."

"Now?" she clapped the book shut, trying to dismiss the moment and the yearning that penetrated her leaking heart.

Here she stood in the nearly completed schoolhouse she'd fought for, and the only thing she wanted was to read a page aloud. So many times she'd envisioned herself teaching here. Why had she ever thought it would be possible... to be normal... to be able to teach the thing she often couldn't do herself?

She was a fraud.

Gabe's watching eyes bore into her expectantly as she fought the cruel affliction he didn't know existed. "Are you all right?"

She'd once thought he was insincere and playing with her affections, but he was the one who was honest and forthright. And he was a romantic who wanted to marry her and soon. The grip of panic tightened the ever-present knot inside her. She took a small step back. "Everything is moving so quickly."

"Quickly?"

"Yes... between us."

He pulled his hand away from the wall and dusted the splinters from it. "I waited years to be with you. When you finally showed some interest, I spoke to your father and got his blessing. That was almost three months ago, Liv. I'm not sure I could move any slower." He groaned. "But I'll do whatever it takes to prove my sincerity."

"No, that's not it. I know you're sincere. It's just that…"
Pressure built behind her eyes as tears threatened to spill. She
looked away from him and toward the front of the room where
her desk would be, where she would stand and teach and
fumble for words when they disappeared from the page, where
her fraudulence would be exposed.

The children deserved a better teacher, and Gabe deserved
a better mate. The least she could do was give him some
warning their courtship would never lead to marriage. "You
have been good to me, patient too, but I wouldn't make a good
wife."

In one swift motion, he stepped close and reached for her
arms. "You would."

"I'm afraid I would not. Nor would I make a good
mother."

"Yes, you would. You're wonderful with children."

"I'm afraid we—"

"No, you aren't afraid of us…" His searing gaze begged to
be met. "Not of our future together. You are afraid of
something. I just haven't figured out what it is, but I will." He
grinned with the sweet self-assurance she used to think was
cockiness. "By the time I finish building these desks, I'll prove
your fear is unfounded."

She blinked back her tears. "And if you can't?"

"I'll start on the bookshelves."

His blithe spirit made her smile, but he had no idea she
was a fraud. The thorn in her side would always remain and
would end her teaching career if discovered. "I will disappoint
everyone, especially now that everything is going ahead with
the school."

"I thought you were happy you are finally getting what
you want."

Unless something somehow assured her that every time
she looked at a page she would be able to read clearly, she
would always be afraid. If she could tell anyone that, it was
Gabe. Some part of her was desperate to, but instead she

forced a half smile. "I am happy. But the further I go in all this, the more likely I am to… disappoint someone."

"Who?"

"I don't know… you."

"You could never disappoint me."

"You don't know everything about me."

"That's what we have our whole lives for."

She held back her tears. "What if you find out everything about me and decide you don't want me after all?"

"Impossible."

"You say that now but—"

"You're wrong." He lowered his chin, and his faint grin deepened. "But if it will help you accept my love, I promise to keep my expectations low so I don't get disappointed."

"Now you are teasing me."

"I'm not. I love you, Liv." He lowered his face to hers. "I can't remember not loving you. That won't change, no matter what comes. Or what you think might come."

His tender words were followed by an even sweeter kiss, smothering her anxiety. Held in his confident embrace, the affection from her heart and the desire from nature swirled into a passion that could not be ignored. She parted her lips, inviting him to deepen the kiss.

He pulled back with a heavy breath.

She opened her eyes. "Did I do something wrong?"

He pressed his forehead against hers. "Heavens, no. You're amazing. Perfect for me." His voice was quiet and gruff. "I shouldn't be alone with you like this one more moment until we are man and wife. Either go with me to the reverend's house to get married this instant or leave me here to work alone."

CHAPTER SEVENTEEN

"I do wish she'd answer quickly," Alice shielded her ruddy face from the frigid wind. "Maybe she didn't hear you knock."

"It's a one-room cabin." Olivia rolled her eyes at her sister and knocked a second time on Marian's door. "She's probably tending to the baby."

The door creaked opened a sliver. Marian squinted out against the cold. Her eyes widened when they landed on Olivia. "Oh, heavens! I'm so sorry," she exclaimed as she flung the door wide. "Do come in. I thought you were Jonah knocking the snow from his boots."

Olivia and Alice stepped inside. Olivia closed the door behind her sister, trying to keep the precious warmth inside Marian's home. "Alice and I spent the morning double-lining our bonnets. It made them divinely cozy, so we did it to these booties for Frederick." She held the tiny baby socks out to Marian.

"How thoughtful of you!" Marian glanced at her son, who was sleeping in his cradle on the other side of the room. "They will keep him warm when we walk to church on Sunday."

Sweat moistened Olivia's forehead. She untied her thickly lined bonnet. "Maybe too warm." After removing her gloves, she lifted the curtain's edge and looked outside. Wind-driven snow made it difficult to see far. "Where is Jonah?"

"He and Doctor Ashton are at the Colburns' house. Little Anthony fell from a horse and broke his arm."

"That happened to Walter when he was a child. He cried all night." Olivia glanced at Alice, who was still standing by the door in her heavy winter coat with her bonnet tied and her gloved hands clasped. "You were just a baby, so you probably don't remember."

Alice shook her head. "We should go back soon."

Olivia returned her attention to Marian. "When did Anthony fall?"

"This morning. Jonah has been gone all day." Marian stepped to the oven. "I baked bread for him to take to Mr. Weathermon on his visit this afternoon. I don't think he will make it home in time to walk to Mr. Weathermon's cabin and return before sunset. I was going to ask Gabe to take it. He usually stops here on his way home from working on the schoolhouse, but he hasn't come by yet either."

Olivia rubbed the warm lining of her bonnet between her fingers. "We will take the bread to Mr. Weathermon."

Alice drew her head back. "You can't be serious."

"Sure, why not? We are bundled warmly and the snow isn't deep. Think of poor Mr. Weathermon out there by the stream all alone."

Alice smirked. "You just want to see if Gabriel is home next door."

"No, there is a lonely, elderly man who needs fresh bread and we are fit to take it to him." Olivia hid her hands in her gloves. "Besides, Gabe's house is hardly next door to Mr. Weathermon. You can't even see Mr. Weathermon's cabin from Gabe's house." The urge for sisterly bickering rose up in Olivia, but she ignored it. She held out her hands to Marian. "I will take it to Mr. Weathermon myself. There is still an hour of daylight left."

Marian cocked her head. "But it is snowing."

"Not badly."

"And windy."

"I'll be fine."

Marian wrapped the hot pan in a towel and passed the bundled bread to Olivia. "Stay on the path. Turn left at the bent pine. Please be careful out there."

"I will," she said and then turned to her sister. "Are you coming with me?"

"Must I?"

"No."

Alice grinned slightly and stepped outside. "Then I shall see you at home."

"Tell Mother I won't be long."

Alice waved to Marian and trotted east toward their family's house.

Snowflakes doused the warmth in Olivia's cheeks as she hurried west on the path through the forest toward the stream. She glanced back once, but couldn't see Marian's cabin for the falling snow. Round, wet flakes clung to one side of the pine branches, creating a shadowy beauty along the path.

The wind increased. Though she couldn't see more than ten yards in any directions, she knew exactly where she was. The open meadow where fawns played in summertime would be on one side and gray leaf trees on the other. She kept a brisk pace through the ankle-deep snow and in less than a quarter hour, the bent trunk of a tall pine appeared to split the path ahead.

Gabe's house was only a few yards to the right, but she couldn't see it. How she wished he were home right now! But he would be working inside the school. She tried to peer through the white wall of snow falling around her and still couldn't see his house or the stream beyond it.

Hugging the warm pan of bread against her coat, she followed the path that veered to the left. Chimney smoke clung to the air. As she hiked between snow-covered hemlock trees, the dark wood of Mr. Weathermon's cabin appeared in front of her. He answered the door quicker than she expected. "Miss Owens?"

The wind momentarily stilled as if frightened by Mr. Weathermon's booming baritone. He leaned his ample figure against a cane and looked down at her disdainfully.

"Yes, sir." She proffered the wrapped pan of bread. "This is from Marian. Jonah is assisting Doctor Ashton, and Gabe is working in the schoolhouse, so I offered to—"

"Come in, girl. Come in." His jowls wobbled as he spoke. "No sense in dawdling at the door and letting the heat out."

Still holding the bread, she stepped inside and gave his cabin a quick glance. Tidy, but cramped. A patchwork quilt neatly swathed a drooping mattress by the curtained window. Clothes and coats hung on pegs, and a full bucket of clean water sat next to the washstand. A bull's horn, an assortment of iron files, and odd shavings covered a square table by the fireplace. Three intricately carved powder horns hung on the wall over the mantel.

"You are dripping," he said, using his cane to mop a towel along the floor from the front door to her feet.

She quickly returned her snowy boots to the mat by the door. "My apologies."

"Not to worry." He pointed at one of two chairs at the table. "Sit yourself down."

"No, I should be getting back."

"You need to warm your boots before you go out in that again." He took the bread from her. "You'll be walking into the wind on your way back. Frightfully cold, I'd expect."

She removed her gloves, which were still warm from holding the bread, and pointed at the ornately carved powder horns on the wall. "Did you make those?"

"Indeed." He slid the bread pan onto the table between a burning oil lamp and a dusty chisel. "Except this one," he said, selecting the furthermost of the three powder horns. "My grandfather used this one during the war."

Olivia stepped closer and stuffed her gloves into her coat pocket. "Which war?"

"Eighteen-twelve. He fought at Fort Madison." Mr. Weathermon ran a finger along the inscrutable letters carved into the horn. "Do you read Latin, girl?"

Though she knew some Latin, at present the letters were a blur. She shook her head, thankful he hadn't asked her to try and read it.

Passing her the horn, he read the phrase. "Ad victoria. It means for victory."

She turned the horn in her hands and followed a line of ivy trailing around the design all the way to the tip. "It's lighter than I expected."

"Because it's empty." He returned the horn to its place on the wall. "I wouldn't dare use it. Not that I'm much for sentiment. It's old, that's all. Might crack."

"I see." She moved close to the table and examined the horn he'd been working on. "How long does it take you to finish one?"

He didn't answer. Why had she expected him to? He'd already said more to her in a few minutes than he had in the entire two years she'd known him.

The intricacy of the details he'd carved astounded her. Such minutely detailed work seemed tedious for a former shipping tycoon. She lowered herself to the chair's edge. "How many of these have you made?"

He sat in the chair opposite her and sliced the bread. "Just those two on the wall and the one you're picking at."

She drew her hand away from his work in progress. "My apologies, sir."

"You've said that twice now, girl." He offered her the first slice, and she took it. "Do you always cower?"

"No, sir. I was being polite."

"Seemed like cowering to me. You don't cower, do you?"

"I hope not."

"You'll have to do better than that," he boomed.

She'd walked in the cold to bring him bread, showed interest in his lonely life, and now he was mocking her. How impertinent! She stood abruptly, her chair screeching on the floor. "Then I retract my polite apology, sir. I'm not sorry I touched it."

He laughed, mouth full of bread. "There's a girl!" He tapped the table with two stubby fingers. "Now sit yourself back down and finish your bread. I can't stand a crumb-dropper any more than a soft sap."

Slowly, she lowered herself to the chair, not in obedience, but in curiosity. "Mr. Weathermon, why did you come here with us? Why settle somewhere new all by yourself at your age?"

"You are a nosy girl, aren't you?"

Resolved not to apologize, she set her uneaten slice of bread back in the pan. "Why did you leave America?"

Unshaken, Mr. Weathermon finished his bread in silence then wiped the crumbs from his fingertips. "I was a fraud. I lived pretending to be something I was not and it led to my failure." He tapped his chest. "And my heart warned me. One heart isn't enough to sustain two people, you see."

"No, I don't."

"I lived as myself and as the person I pretended to be. It was too much for one heart." He rested his heavy arms on the table. "Doctor Ashton and I were old chums and once he confirmed my condition was mild, he suggested I come out here with you all."

She searched for an explanation. "For the fresh air?"

"That and to enjoy my retirement in peace." He grinned and for a moment he reminded her of her grandfather.

"Fair enough," she said raising her bread slice as if congratulating him. As Mr. Weathermon ate, he told her about his carvings, picking berries, living near Gabe, and his hope she wouldn't mind having an old man around from time to time once she and Gabe married.

"Of course, not," she said as she rose from the table. "If we marry."

"You will, girl. You will."

While he continued speaking, she unwrapped her heavy shawl and checked the time on her silver watch pin. "It stopped."

"Pardon?"

"I must have forgotten to wind my watch." She lifted the curtain, but a thin sheet of ice covered the outside of the glass. "Any idea of the time?"

"Probably past time for you to get back." Mr. Weathermon stood slowly. "Here, take a lantern." He took a lantern from a shelf by the door, struck a match, and held the light out to her. "Take care getting home. And thank you for bringing the bread."

She tied on her warm bonnet and accepted the lantern, pinching its wire handle. "It was my pleasure, Mr. Weathermon."

"Give my thanks to Marian," he boomed from his doorstep.

She marched into the bitter cold and called over her shoulder, "I will."

The thud of his cabin door closing sent a fresh clump of snow from his roof to the ground behind her. She picked up her pace. Her boots crunched the snow down the incline from his cabin, which seemed steeper on the way down than it had on the way here.

She hadn't meant to stay at Mr. Weathermon's house for so long. Thick clouds suffocated the last light of day, bringing an early night. What she'd thought was going to be a light snowfall had turned into a blizzard. It felt nothing like her first two winters in Good Springs—one with frequent light snows, and the other a mix of mild days and sporadic heavy snowfall.

The white of the snow all around created a false sense of light. She glanced back at where Mr. Weathermon's cabin stood, but couldn't see more than ten foot behind her. Snow fell rapidly, its flakes both boisterous and benign.

Shrill wind thrashed her face, tugging on her bonnet. She stopped walking long enough to set the lantern down, turn her back to the wind, and tuck her shawl higher around her neck. Holding the woolen mass tightly around her neck with one hand, she lifted the lantern.

The flame trembled inside its glass encasement.

"Don't go out on me now," she encouraged the little light as she held it up.

She'd hoped to retrace her footprints home, but the snowstorm left only faint ovals in the rising snow. The closer she looked at the white ripples on the path, the less they looked like footprints. She searched the ground around her. Snow blanketed the forest floor in monotonous sheets between the trees all around her. She might not be on the path at all.

A blinding wall of blowing snow trapped her on all sides. The wind was on her back when she'd left Marian's, so if she kept walking into it, she should be going in the right direction. Snowflakes nestled in her lashes and her eyes begged to close against the bitter chill. She would not let them close. She would press on and keep moving.

Her boots grew heavier with each step as the snow packed around the soles. The harder she hiked, the warmer her head became, but with each heavy breath, icy air stung the back of her throat. Wind rumbled the snow in maddening waves like the pelting grain from a thresher's blade. Beneath the groan and pleas of the snow-drenched forest, water trickled nearby.

She stopped and listened.

Willing her shivering arm to hold the lantern farther from her body, she searched the area around her but saw nothing except white whirls and sticks. But now the brutal wind was at her back. She'd turned somehow. Or the wind had changed. It was toying with her, taunting her, luring her to a cold and pointless death.

How had this happened?

The snowflakes that had caught in the folds of her shawl near her neck melted and soaked her collar. Her cuffs were wet too, drawing heat out of her blood. Her fingers were stiffening around the lantern handle. She tried to switch the lantern to the other hand, but her fingers refused to move correctly. The lantern slipped her gasped, and the snow swallowed it whole.

"No!" Her cry dissolved on the relentless wind. She dug for the lantern, ignoring the sting of snow as it slithered into her gloves. As she pulled the lantern from its alabaster grave, she took a step back and sank her boot into the edge of the stream. Water seeped into her shoe faster than she could yank her foot from the mud. How had she come so close to the stream and not known it? Maybe this wasn't the big stream, but a brook leading to it.

Blinded by the snow and deafened by the wind, she dropped the useless lantern and moved forward, holding her head down and one hand out. "Please, God, lead me to safety." The words slipped from her chattering lips as she pressed forward, following her boot prints away from the water. Only when she stepped in one print did the next print come into view.

Her wet and tingling toes felt numb inside her ice-laden boots. If she could make it back to Mr. Weathermon's home, she would be fine. His cabin was warm, and he was far more amiable than she'd expected. He would shelter her for the night. With each step she thought of her family, her students, the community that needed her, the new schoolhouse she'd worked so hard for, Gabe...

Marian had said Gabe was working in the schoolhouse. He would have seen the blizzard coming and possessed better sense than to walk home in these conditions. He'd probably gone to his family's house for the night. Maybe he would come looking for her in the morning. They all would. And there she'd lie, frozen and blue, the senseless word blind teacher girl.

No! She could not think that way. Her aching feet found one more boot print to follow, then another. She would make it back to Mr. Weathermon's and have a harrowing tale to tell. He'd scoff at her, but years from now, on a cold and windy night, children would ask her to recount the time she'd gotten lost in the blizzard. They would gather around and turn the lamps down low while she told the story slowly, hoping to scare them into having a better fear of the elements than she'd had.

Her old footprints became harder to decipher, each one more blown and buried than the last. The wind carried a faint whiff of smoke, but from where?

Her trembling muscles burned deep inside. She forced each step until no more prints were visible. Reaching her hands out in all directions, she found a tree trunk. Her quaking knees gave out and she fell against the rough pine bark. She walked her hands along the bark, trying to get a grip and pull herself up, but the trunk curved unnaturally. Her hands followed the bend in the trunk. It was the bent pine tree marking the split in the path. She was close to Gabe's cabin. He wouldn't be there, but if she could make it inside, she could light the fire and survive the night.

The unflinching wind beat against her as she clung to the tree. Her body refused to move. It shook violently from within, sickening her exhausted frame.

"Gabe!" she called, knowing he wouldn't hear. "Gabe!" Her burning voice cried again and again. Knowing it might be her last word, she gathered every ounce of air in her lungs and tried again. "Gabriel!"

A clap resounded nearby. Fearing a snow-laden limb had cracked, she curled her arms around her legs and cowered close to the bent pine. A rhythmic swishing sound repeated beneath the harsh drone of the wind. The sound grew louder, closer.

"Liv?" A voice called. "Olivia? Say something if you can hear me."

"Over here." Her voice broke as she tried to yell. "Gabe! I'm by the bent pine."

Hearing boots crunch snow in rapid stride, she tried to stand. Her cold knees wouldn't straighten, her skirts stiffened with ice.

Gabe scooped her from the snow. "I've got you," he said as he lifted her away from the bent pine.

The slanted line of falling snow went vertical. She buried her face against his warm shoulder as he carried her to his cabin. His woolen coat smelled of lumber and soap and wood smoke and man. Heat radiated from his neck. He'd been inside by a roaring fire, not walking home in the blizzard, not working at the schoolhouse.

His steady and confident stride made her feel foolish for getting lost in the first place. He could see fine in the dark or he knew the way so well the wind and snow didn't disorient him. These were his woods.

Allowing her eyes to close, she tried to relax in his arms. A moment later, he stopped abruptly and pushed a door open. The warmth inside his house tingled her icy cheeks. She tried to speak but her shivering jaw felt anchored shut.

He set her down on a block chair just inside the door of the lamp lit kitchen. "Get your boots off."

When he closed the door, the wind lost its deadly grip on her soul. The scent of stew added to the warmth. "Gabe…" she hummed, content simply to be indoors. "Thank you."

"They look wet." He arched a worried eyebrow at her feet as he shook the snow from his coat and hung it on a peg by the door. "Are they wet?"

"Hm?"

"Your boots, your stockings? Are they wet?"

She reached for her shoelaces, but her frozen fingers wouldn't pinch the ends to untie them. "So cold."

Gabe dropped to his knees in front of her and quickly untied the leather laces. Panic edged his voice. "How long were you out there?"

"I d-don't know. A while."

He gripped her shin with one warm hand and used the other to tug off her wet boot. "Liv, your skin is freezing."

She didn't want to think about frozen things or look at her icy clothes or ever hear the wind again. She cast her gaze about the messy room. Though it was meant to serve as a kitchen someday, it lacked a table and stove. A fluffy new mattress—the handiwork of Mrs. Ashton no doubt—lay on the floor near the stone hearth of the fireplace her father and Walter had built. She knew Gabe was living in his house while he finished it and worked on the school, but she'd never imagined what that would look like.

But at present, it was hard to imagine anything. A wave of fatigue dropped her head back against the wall. "I can't feel my toes."

"Why were you walking in a blizzard?"

"I took bread to Mr. Weathermon."

"You shouldn't have in this weather."

Her teeth ached from chattering. "It was b-barely snowing when I left Marian's."

"Jonah should have stopped you."

"I'm a grown woman—"

"Who almost got herself killed," he interrupted with his volume raised. "You are freezing. Your lips are blue. Your clothes are covered in ice and snow. What were you thinking?"

She pulled her head away from the wall. "Why are you angry?"

"I'm not angry." He peeled her frozen stocking from her skin and then took off the other boot. His voice softened. "This foot is worse than the other."

"I stepped in water." She looked at her hands. Melting snow caked the folds of her black leather gloves. She tried to pull them off one finger at a time but moved too slowly for Gabe's concern.

Without a word, he took her hands and slid the gloves off her icy fingers. "Oh, Olivia, no."

"What?"

He rubbed her hands in his and blew hot air into them. "We have to warm you up."

"I'm f-fine, really."

"Look at your feet."

"They're white."

"Too white." He traced a finger across the top of her foot. "Can you feel this?"

"No."

He unwrapped the crackly shawl from her shoulders. "Take your coat off."

"Won't I warm up faster if I stay bundled?"

"No. It's wet. Take it off," he ordered as he tossed her shawl to the top of a trunk, "and your dress."

The improper suggestion snapped her alert. "I beg your pardon?"

"Your virtue isn't at stake here, but your health is."

"What will people think?"

"That I saved your life." The gravity of his care kept his eyes dark and the line between his lips straight. "Your wet clothes are leeching the heat out of your body." He moved to the fireplace and added logs to the blaze. "I'll go and find you some clean clothes, but for now take off everything that's wet, leave it by the door, and wrap yourself under there." He pointed to the mass of quilts on the mattress by the hearth. "Feet nearest the fire. I'll be right back."

As he started for the staircase, she managed a rigid nod and waited for him to disappear upstairs before she began undressing. Though her fingers had lost most of their dexterity, she forced them to work the buttons. There was no way she'd ask him to undress her. After a moment of struggle, her dress and petticoat dropped to the floor. She left them in a melting heap by the door and scurried to the mattress by the hearth, wearing only her undergarments.

The wide and soft mattress enveloped her like a fresh pastry. She tugged one of the quilts over her shivering body and laid her head on the pillow. His pillow. The mattress smelled like him and also faintly like the Ashtons' cinnamon-scented home. The mattress hadn't been here long—probably part of a trade for the work Gabe had done on their house.

She pulled the quilt up to her ears and stretched her feet down the mattress toward the hearth, like he'd told her to. The bed's temperature matched the room, but it was still warmer than her skin. She swished her legs on the bedsheet to create warmth, but exhausted quickly. When she went still, the only sound in the house came from pops and crackles of the fire.

Footsteps descended the stairs, but Olivia didn't look. She'd have to crane her neck, and her aching head was close to comfortable on the pillow.

"Here's a clean night shirt," he said, setting a folded flannel garment on the corner of the mattress. "And a pair of ridiculously long socks my sister knitted for me years ago." The socks unfolded as he held them up by the cuffs.

"You're right."

"Long, aren't they?"

"And ridiculous."

He grinned, looking like himself for a moment—causal, open, confident, alluring. A man she could easily spend her life with. His serious expression quickly returned, as did the urgency in his movements. He shook open a second quilt, covered her with it, and tucked it around her the way a parent tucks in a child.

She watched his face as he rubbed her feet. He'd saved her life tonight. She was safe with him. Safe to love him. Safe to let him love her. But even though her heart knew it, her mind refused to give up its guard.

A strange sensation tingled the soles of her feet. Before she could say anything, her toes and the skin on top of her feet felt as if she were being pricked with one thousand needles. With a sharp wince, she sat up and curled her feet into her body.

Gabe's hands shot up. "What's wrong?"

She held the quilt to her chin with one hand and squeezed her stinging feet with the other. "Pins and needles."

He lowered his hands. "That's a good thing."

"It doesn't feel good."

"It means you're getting the feeling back."

"Oh, good." She relaxed a little, but felt silly. She sent him a rueful smile. "So, I will live after all?"

His grin returned. "Yeah, you will live."

CHAPTER EIGHTEEN

On Olivia's last day teaching in the Cotter house, she had to fold her excited hands behind her back to keep them still. When her hands went still, her stomach fluttered. Glee from the happy anticipation of never having to come back to this house mixed with dread from the hateful glares of the older Cotter girls.

If only little Jane and Conrad would finish their exam quickly so she could collect their papers and leave. She hadn't been able to read a word all morning and there was no way she'd be able to read their handwritten exams here now.

Peggy sat in a kitchen chair. She focused on her lace-making cushion, seeming blissfully ignorant of her sisters' rude behavior nearby. Her fingers left the lace long enough to smooth her perfectly quaffed hair. She flashed Olivia a pretty smile. "I declare you are a good schoolteacher."

"That's very gracious," Olivia whispered, hoping Peggy would take the hint and keep her voice down until the children were done writing.

She considered Peggy's kind remark. Such words were infrequent from her these days. It wasn't always that way. Peggy was once one of her dearest friends, not simply for lack of options, as it seemed since coming to this land. When they were girls—before the drive to get male attention overtook Peggy's manners—they often spent the night at each other's houses, staying up late, giggling and playing. Olivia missed the freedom in friendship that made those times enjoyable. She glanced back at Peggy and whispered. "I appreciate your saying so."

One of the older girls snickered at her from the kitchen. The three of them whispered to each other then went out the back door. Olivia didn't relax until the door closed behind them. They met Mrs. Cotter in the yard. Peggy returned her attention to her lace.

Olivia thanked God it was her last day here. She'd never expected a family who was once close to hers to be the dread of her week. Though Mr. Cotter was an elder and a good man, he was busy building his stables and breeding horses and teaching the work to his eldest son. Mrs. Cotter had changed the most and seemed to have taken three of her five daughters with her on the path to unrighteousness. Perhaps Olivia could be a strong enough influence in Jane's life that she might remain the one Cotter woman capable of dependable kindness.

Jane laid down her pencil, regaining Olivia's attention. "Are you finished with your exam, Jane?" she asked.

Jane nodded.

"Excellent. Sit quietly and wait for your brother to finish," she whispered. "This is how it will be when we are all in the schoolhouse together next week."

A few minutes later, Conrad smacked his pencil on his paper. "Done!" he exclaimed, dropping both arms as if answering the essay question had taken away all of his strength.

Olivia collected the children's papers. "I'll grade these tonight and see you in class next Monday."

"Thank you, Miss Owens," the children said in practiced unison and dashed outside to play.

Peggy stood from the kitchen chair and fluffed the ruffles at her sleeves. The smell of feminine power clung to the air around her. She lowered her dainty fingers to the table and picked up Jane's exam paper. "My, she has come a long way with your teaching."

"Yes, I'm very proud of her." Olivia collected Conrad's paper and pencil and waited for Peggy to hand her the other exam.

"Look how sweet. She wrote that her favorite animal in the settlement is the jackrabbit because… something about its ears…" Peggy pointed a knuckle at a word on the paper. "What did she write here?"

"I don't know. I'll grade it tonight."

"No, look at it now." Peggy's tone threatened a pout. "I want to know what she wrote."

"I'm not sure what it says. She's still learning cursive. I will have to take a closer look tonight when I have time."

Peggy tilted her chin and studied Olivia for a moment. She looked at the paper again then raised an eyebrow. "Oh wait, I see what it says. Gracious, isn't that the dearest thing! Read this part."

Olivia flicked a glance at the inscrutable markings. "Yes, Jane is darling."

"You didn't read it."

"Of course I did."

"Then what does it say?"

Olivia swiped the paper from Peggy's flimsy grip and studied the marks on the page. She couldn't make out a single word. "She likes the jackrabbit's ears."

"I can't believe it!" Peggy covered her mouth with her hand. "You can't read, can you?"

Olivia's fluttering stomach sank. Her chest felt hollow without it as if she had hidden her darkest secret within her retreating vital organs. She tried to bolster her voice. "What gave you that idea?"

"You are holding the paper upside down." A wicked grin curved one edge of Peggy's mouth and every ounce of beauty drained from her face. "After all of these years, I finally figured out what is so odd about you. You're illiterate."

"No, I'm not." She reached for her satchel. "I'm in a hurry, that's all. I must get to the Vestals'. I have to complete the examinations this week so I know where to begin our lessons as a class next week."

Peggy inched closer. "Now that I think of it, you were always helping your mother with the other students in class, and making excuses for not reading aloud. You were actually getting them to read the words for you, weren't you?"

Her thoughts scrambled for a defense, but all that came out was a stunted whisper. "I can read."

Peggy cackled as she snatched the paper and flipped it right side up. "Then read this."

Olivia would have grabbed her satchel and hurried out of the house, but her breath caught, her mind froze, and her pulse rang in her ears. The letters on the page resembled honeysuckle blowing on a scrolling vine more than words. "I can't."

Peggy's voice cooed in mock sympathy. "Perhaps it is your eyesight? How many fingers am I holding up?"

"Don't be cruel."

"Maybe you're going blind."

"I can see just fine."

"Then why can't you read this?"

"I don't know."

Peggy propped both fists on her corset-cinched waist. "Can you read at all?"

"Of course I can. Sometimes I just can't see words."

"What does that mean?"

Despite her racing heartbeat, she found the strength to coolly pack her satchel. "Forget it. You wouldn't understand."

Peggy leaned forward. "I'd like to try."

"Why?"

"Because I'm your friend."

Olivia almost swallowed her tongue. "My friend? You were my friend. But something changed. You changed. You made me feel ugly and unwanted. I trusted you and you filled my head with lies."

"Not so!"

"You've been lying to me about Gabe for years."

"To protect you from him."

"He has sincerely loved me since I was fifteen. You made me believe he couldn't be trusted. You told me he laughed about me behind my back when really he loves me."

Peggy's top lip twitched and her voice rose with shrill volume. "He told me he loved me once too, and he's been flirting with Frances and with Cecelia."

Olivia stabbed a finger toward Peggy. "I don't believe you anymore."

"He tried to kiss me."

"Ha! That's definitely a lie. Gabe doesn't try to kiss."

Peggy's eyes widened. "Well, it doesn't matter. He won't want you when he finds out you can't read and you have been faking it all this time. What man would love a woman who lives a lie? In fact, I think the elders need to know about this. The little teacher girl who has been challenging all the parents over education can't even read."

"I can read... I can't always see letters, but I manage just fine."

Peggy tapped a finger to her lip, faking deliberation. "Still, I should probably do my civic duty and let the elders know the truth about you."

Nervous bile bubbled up in Olivia's throat. Her mouth opened and she feared she might retch across the Cotters' kitchen table. Instead, her voice filled with the strength of anger. "You do and I will expose your mother for the thief she is."

Peggy gasped and stepped backward with her lace-covered wrists propped on her hips. "She is not a thief! My mother has never stolen anything in her life."

"I saw her," Olivia hissed, finally having leverage. "Mr. Vestal and I watched her try to break into their barn. When she couldn't get in, she went for their chicken coop. She's been stealing from them and did the same to us for months."

Peggy picked at her fluffy cuffs. "Ah yes, you and Mr. Vestal. I've seen you two strolling along the lane together. He is probably waiting on the road for you now. He seems quite smitten with you."

"I'm teaching his children."

"Does Gabe know?"

"Of course."

"That Mr. Vestal is in love with you?"

"He isn't… not like that…" So much for leverage. Why had she thought she could beat Peggy at her own game? The more she tried, the deeper she sank. She gave Peggy a solid stare and walked out. "Just keep your mouth shut."

Peggy squared her shoulders with smug satisfaction. "Then you had better forget what you think you saw my mother do." Her voice returned to a feminine but fake politeness before she closed the door. "You have a lot more to lose than I do."

CHAPTER NINETEEN

Olivia lost a full night's sleep. She yawned as she gouged her chignon with hairpins to secure it for an afternoon of teaching. Faint circles haunted the skin under her eyes, attesting to her insomnia. She could make it through her afternoon lessons with the McIntosh children then get a quick nap before dinner.

Icy wind whipped into the Owenses' kitchen and up the stairs. Olivia ran down to the open door and almost yelled out to her young brother, but Richie was already halfway across the frozen yard.

She draped her winter shawl over her shoulders and grabbed the strap of her satchel. She didn't have time for this, but no one else was left in the house, and she couldn't let Richie get away with leaving the door open when it was below freezing outside. She affected her voice with the schoolteacher tone she'd been practicing. "Richard Junior, get back here this instant!"

Richie halted in the yard and turned back, eyes downcast.

Olivia's cold toes curled in her socks. She stepped away from the threshold as Richie approached the porch. "You left the door wide open." She reached for her boots. "You must close the door behind you or the warm air escapes."

Richie licked his chapped lips and stared at her feet. "Sorry."

She had to get to the McIntosh house to teach, but her little brother's nose was running. She waved him inside. "Where is your handkerchief?" she asked as she sat to pull on her boots.

He didn't answer.

She dropped her boots without looking at them and felt his coat pocket. It was empty except for a hard lump with a pointed end. She stuck her hand into his pocket and pulled out their mother's sewing scissors. "What are you doing with these?"

Richie's chin scrunched into a dimpled mass, and his bottom lip began to quiver. He pointed at her boots on the floor. "I'm sorry, Livy."

Her leather shoelaces had been cut clean through. She fingered the nubs of leather cord poking uselessly from the lace holes on her boots. "What have you done?"

"I said I'm sorry."

She slapped the scissors onto the table. "Richie, it is freezing outside and I still have to walk to the McIntoshes to teach. I don't have any more cord to use for laces. How could you do something so harmful? If you keep this up, we won't have anything left in this house. Have you cut anything else I need to know about?"

When he looked up at her, speechless, she touched her hair and gasped. "It was you!"

Richie backed away and his face reddened. "Please don't be mad at me, Livy. I can't help it."

Olivia dropped into the chair, exasperated. Her little brother had been the one who cut her braid while she had slept that day. He was her assailant.

While Richie sobbed like any nine-year-old caught in his mischief, Olivia's tears welled up too. She covered her face with her hands. "I can't believe this. On top of everything else I have to deal with, I can't trust my little brother."

"I'll never do it again." Richie inched closer. His young crying voice sounded like their sisters. "Please say you forgive me."

She blinked away her tears to clear her vision. "Richie, I forgive you, but I don't understand why you did that to me... to my hair... and my boots."

"I don't know why. I just like to cut things."

"I must tell Father and Mother."

"No, please no. I'll stop."

"We can't trust you." She pulled a kerchief from her sleeve and wiped his nose. "We didn't bring much with us from America. There are no mail order companies here or stores where we can purchase more goods. We must take care of everything we have and be diligent to make more. Everyone is working as hard as they can. You can't ruin things that don't belong to you."

"I won't do it anymore. Am I going to be in trouble?"

"That is up to Father."

"Can I still go to school on Monday? I won't cut things in class, I promise."

"In class..." She hadn't thought of that. He would have to be watched constantly to make sure he wasn't playing with scissors or knives or whatever implement he found to satisfy his destructive compulsion. What if he cut one of the other students' hair or chopped up the pages of their precious books?

This was sinister behavior for an otherwise normal boy. He needed to be counseled and disciplined beyond her ability. What if the other children brought problems like this to class too? How could she possibly teach a school full of misbehaving children? What had she been thinking of working so hard for a responsibility she wasn't prepared for?

"I don't know if you will be allowed to go to school or not." She pulled on her unlaced boots. "Father is in the barn. I'll take you to him then I have to get to the McIntosh house for lessons. No matter what Father says, you promised me you would stop cutting things that don't belong to you, and I expect you to keep your promise."

* * *

Olivia's unlaced boots flopped as she trudged through the cold wind to the McIntosh house. The afternoon sky darkened more by the minute, promising icy rain, maybe snow. As she approached the house, Gabe stepped out to the porch, and everything felt right again. Even Richie's behavior couldn't suppress her smile now. "Hello," she said.

Gabe gave a short nod, but no smile or greeting.

Olivia raised one floppy boot to the porch step and stopped short. "What's wrong?"

Barnabus stepped out the door behind Gabe. He waved to Olivia. Gabe signed *wait inside* to his younger brother. The little boy looked to her for confirmation. Olivia signed *one moment*. Barnabus nodded and went back into the house to wait for his lessons. Warm air escaped the house before the door closed and he slipped inside.

Olivia wanted to follow him into the cozy house, but something wasn't right with Gabe. Once the door closed, she stepped close to the man she loved. "Has something happened?"

Gabe sank his hands into his coat pockets. "You tell me." His gruff voice betrayed his anger.

She glanced into the house through the window behind him. Barnabus and the other McIntosh children were inside, getting their books and slates ready. Nothing appeared to be wrong. "I don't understand."

Gabe spoke quietly through barely parted lips. "After all of these years that I have pursued you... and loved you... it is unfair to make me compete with someone else for your affections."

"Compete for my affections?"

"I know about you and Mr. Vestal."

"Christopher?"

Gabe's nostrils flared. "Yes, Christopher. Peggy told me all about it. Your long walks together and how you..." his Adam's apple raised and lowered as he paused to swallow, "you stay at his house late into the night."

Though only the icy wind moved through the porch, the earth seemed to spin around her. Her chest tightened, stealing the air from her lungs. Everything seemed to be in motion at once.

Everything but Gabe.

He stood straight and tall like a boulder in a raging torrent. He had built desire in her just as he'd built the schoolhouse and his home and he'd assured her it could be hers with every nail he'd driven. He'd promised she wouldn't disappoint him and with one word from Peggy, it was all washing away.

She wanted to reach out and hang onto him and allow his strength to sustain her as her world melted, but he was the one eroding the earth from beneath her feet. She couldn't touch him, so she leaned a gloved hand onto the porch railing to steady herself. "It's not like that... Christopher and I..."

He flinched. "Are you in love with him?"

"No. Why would you—"

"Is he in love with you? That would certainly explain why he praises your teaching so highly during the elder meetings."

She drew her head back. "So the only reason a man might say I'm a good teacher is if he is in love with me?"

"You tell me. How long has this been going on? Has he told you he loves you?"

His questions came faster than she could think. She opened her mouth to speak but couldn't answer.

"Well?" He probed. "Has he asked you to marry him?"

It was true that Christopher had proposed marriage—not because they were in love, as Peggy had made Gabe believe, but it was still true. Olivia had to be honest. If the truth had the power to set her free, why did she feel like she was opening a vile of poison? The truth would kill her and she had no choice but to drink it.

Her answer came on a hopeless whisper. "Yes, he asked me to marry him."

The cavernous space between them grew. Gabe's blue eyes darkened to gray, matching the dark clouds billowing over the settlement. "What was your answer?"

"I refused him."

"Have you been toying with his affections?"

"No. Of course not."

"Are you toying with mine?"

"No."

Anger emanated from him like the heat off a toxic flame. Everything in her body told her to step back from this hurt and angry man, but there was nowhere to go from here. If he believed Peggy over her, their relationship was hopeless. She'd never wanted to fall in love, and she'd once thought she could end this herself if she had to. Standing before him, faced with the possibility of losing him, she knew there was no turning back. It was either a life with Gabriel McIntosh or a life spent in misery. Her love for him had broken her ability to hope for anything else.

Her feet wanted to turn and run home in her unlaced boots. Her pride told her to square her shoulders and go into the house to teach the McIntosh children. But her heart kept her there. No matter how angry he was, he wouldn't hurt her. Ever.

She stepped closer. "Christopher Vestal wanted a replacement for his wife. I have no intention of being her. He asked me to marry him to help take care of his family. He said he admires me and could see himself falling in love with me if I married him. He is grieving and lonely, and I felt very badly for him when I refused his proposal. He didn't know about you and me."

Gabe raked his fingers through his hair and his expression softened slightly. "He cares about you, Liv, and he is an elder.

I have to work with him on village business for the rest of our lives. I don't want there to be animosity between us."

"We've spoken frankly about his proposal and my relationship with you. He understands. He wishes me the best... with you."

Icy rain began pelleting the ground behind her. Gabe cast his gaze across the wet yard. When he drew his hands out of his pockets, she took another step toward him. "You have no competition for my affections. You told me you love me, and I love you too. I should have told you sooner. It's not fair that I've kept my feelings hidden from you, but I learned a long time ago it's sometimes better to hide things than to be hurt."

A faint grin deepened the lines in the dark stubble around his mouth. He shook his head slowly with his eyes lightening. "No, Liv, it's not better to hide anything—not from me."

The constriction in her chest began to release. "How long have you been stewing over this?"

"Peggy came to me last night."

"Why did you believe her?"

Gabe shrugged and took one of her hands in both of his. "I knew you were hiding something. I used to think it was just some girlish insecurity, but when Peggy came to me about this... it made sense. She has a convincing way of lying."

"Doesn't she though! She told me you tried to kiss her."

His grin disappeared. "She's got it backward."

"Oh?"

"*She* tried to kiss *me*." He groaned and rolled his eyes. "Why would she do this to us?"

"Because she wanted to try to ruin me first."

"First?"

She had to tell him about Mrs. Cotter. He'd said not to hide things from her, so she wouldn't. She tightened her shawl around her cold neck. "Christopher and I discovered Mrs. Cotter has been stealing. He wanted time to think and pray about how to approach her, so we haven't said anything to anyone. But when Peggy discovered my secret yesterday and threatened to tell the elders, I said if she did, I would expose her mother. I guess Peggy thought if she came to you first, no one would believe me."

"When she discovered your secret? Do you mean about Mr. Vestal?"

"No, about… something else."

He gave her hand a light squeeze. "I don't want to hear any more about you from other people, Liv. Tell me now what you've been hiding."

"I can't."

"I love you." He took both of her hands in his. "You can tell me anything. You said you wanted to be fair with me. Since I want to spend my life with you, you have to tell me what is going on. If it affects you, it will affect me."

She stared at her hands, which were swallowed by his. Could she tell him? Trust him? Since someone deceitful in the village already knew her secret, it would be comforting to have someone who loved her on her side. She closed her eyes. "My eyesight is sometimes sort of… impaired. There is no medical term for the condition. I can see everything clearly, but sometimes I cannot see letters or words. I've had it my whole life, but it comes and goes. When I was a child, I imagined there was a monster that put its hand in front of words so I couldn't see them. It took me twice as long as the other children to learn to read, and I was only able to because when I could read, I worked twice as hard."

She opened her eyes and studied Gabe's expression. Where she expected to see disdain, she only saw concern. "What did your parents say about it?"

"I never told them. My father always acted like he was disappointed in me anyway because I wasn't a boy, so I didn't want to give him more reasons."

"What about your mother? She was the teacher."

"She was too busy to notice."

His voice filled with compassion. "Did you ever talk to the doctor about it?"

"When I was ten, I finally got the courage to go to Doctor Ashton. He said there was nothing wrong with my eyes or my vision. He assured me it was no monster, but I still think of it that way sometimes. He is the only person who knows. He said he'd read of things like it and it's just how my mind behaves. He said people would treat me differently my whole life if they knew and it was best if I keep it to myself." Her shoulders rose to her ears as she waited for Gabe to reject her. "It's just how I am. I'm a schoolteacher who can't always read. If the elders find out, they will end my teaching career. Peggy said the same thing, but instead of being my confidant, she's decided to try to ruin me."

Gabe pulled her into his arms. "This isn't your fault and certainly nothing to be ashamed of."

"You're wrong. They wouldn't let me teach if they knew. Teaching is all I want to do. I worked so hard for this. I don't want these children to grow up uneducated or to take their sight and ability to read for granted. People who don't have this difficulty have no idea how grateful they should be. They can't imagine what it's like to be able to read one minute and not the next." She let her face rest against his lapel. "No one can ever know about this."

"They don't need to know. You're a good teacher, and you have proven it."

"Peggy will tell."

"I won't let her."

She pulled back and looked up at him. "Don't go to her about this. Please."

"I don't want her coming between us ever again. I will protect you. I will stand up for you, through this and whatever lies before us."

"You don't have to fix this for me."

He lowered his chin. "Do you trust me?"

"Yes, but please don't go talk to her alone. I don't trust her."

"All right... but I must go to Christopher Vestal."

"About me?"

"No, about Mrs. Cotter stealing. Look at the division this is already causing. Her sin must be exposed. If Christopher agrees with me, we will go to Teddy Cotter together."

"What if Mr. Cotter already knows?"

"He doesn't. I know Teddy and he wouldn't let his wife steal."

"What if she denies it?"

"We will take her before the elders."

All hope for justice dissolved into discouragement. Her shoulders slumped. "That will take weeks."

"No, it won't. This will be over today. I'm going to become an elder here someday, and you will have to trust me to take care of the business God has given me. Just as this settlement trusts you to do the work He has given you." He let go of her hands and glanced into the window at his waiting siblings. "Go and teach the children. I will take care of Mrs. Cotter."

She'd told him the truth and he wanted to help her. She stepped toward the door. Her warm breath flowed freely in wispy white puffs. He'd said her impairment wasn't her fault. As she reached for the handle, she realized he hadn't said if it had changed his feelings for her. She swallowed hard and glanced back at him. "Are you disappointed in me?"

A slow grin reached his eyes. "No, never. I would have preferred if you told me all of this from the beginning, but I understand why you didn't."

"I mean about my word blindness. You deserve someone perfect."

"You are perfect for me."

"But I'm not perfect."

"Nor am I." He tilted his head. "True perfection awaits us in eternity, Liv. Nothing here will come close."

CHAPTER TWENTY

Olivia grabbed Christopher Vestal's sleeve, halting him before he climbed the chapel's stone steps. "I can't do this."

He stopped with one foot hovering over the bottom step. "You must. We must."

She checked the empty road behind them. "I should wait out here for Gabe."

"He asked me to see you inside the chapel while we wait for him and Reverend Colburn to escort Mr. and Mrs. Cotter here. They won't be long." He pointed his thumb toward the arched wooden door at the top of the chapel steps. "The rest of the elders are already in there."

"I know. That's why I can't go in yet. I need to know what happened." Though the air was cold, she fanned her sweaty face with her hands. "How did Mrs. Cotter react when you and Gabe confronted her?"

Christopher glanced around the churchyard. He kept his volume low. "She denied it, and when her denial turned to throwing insults, Gabe and I took the matter to the reverend."

"What did the reverend say?"

"He asked me to gather the elders while he and Gabe went to get Mr. and Mrs. Cotter." Christopher gently took her arm and walked her up the stairs. "And to have you seated before Mrs. Cotter arrives. Something isn't right about Cora these days, and for some reason, she is blaming you for her problems. We will keep you safe. Come inside with me now, please."

As her hand passed over the wooden railing, she remembered the fire on the first day of school. She had stood at the top of these steps and watched Benjamin Foster run to the grove to hide. He had been blamed for starting the fire, and she'd been blamed for it happening while she was in charge. She stopped Christopher once more. "You said it was too early in the morning to start a fire with a magnifying glass."

He raised an eyebrow. "Pardon?"

"The morning of the fire. Benjamin Foster was blamed because everyone saw him by the lumber pile. He had a magnifying glass and we assumed he started the fire, but I remember you saying the sun wouldn't have been high enough. Benjamin never answered questions about it, but you told me it wasn't him." She remembered seeing Mrs. Cotter on the road watching the blaze. "She was there... Mrs. Cotter. She had sent Jane and Conrad to school but kept the other children home because they were working for her. I remember thinking it was odd that they were too busy with work to leave the house, but she was in the village that morning. Do you think she did it?"

"Possibly. But that is not why we're here."

"If Benjamin was falsely accused, we need to apologize to him."

"We will. Let's get through this first."

She followed Christopher to the front pew in the lamp-lit chapel. He held an open palm to the seat and waited politely for her to sit first. As she sat, she studied the faces of the men who were waiting to hear the case against Mrs. Cotter.

Olivia's father watched her with solemn eyes. Doctor Ashton leaned across the pew and gave Christopher's shoulder a supportive squeeze. Jonah and Henry sat in the pew behind the elders, both wearing grave expressions unsuitable for men so young. Mr. McIntosh glanced continually out the window, waiting to see Gabe and Reverend Colburn return with the Cotters.

Though Olivia wanted Mrs. Cotter to be held accountable for her crime, she never thought she would be a witness in Good Springs' first trial. And the person she had to testify against was an unstable woman who probably knew her secret. She clenched her nervous fists.

Christopher looked at her hands then up at her eyes. He leaned close. "Have courage. The truth will set us all free."

They were thinking of two different matters; he was focused on testifying against the thief, but she was filled with dread of being exposed for the sham of a teacher she was. She forced her hands to open, but they tingled deep inside. "Yes... the truth."

The few whispers in the room ceased when Reverend Colburn entered the chapel with Mr. and Mrs. Cotter behind him and Gabe behind them. Mr. Cotter took off his felt hat and wrapped his arm supportively over Mrs. Cotter's back. He probably had no idea how much his wife had stolen and for how long.

Gabe closed the door, sealing them all inside. Olivia glanced at the window and briefly considered jumping headlong through the windowpane. Bits of glass would cling to her dress as she ran across the meadow toward the grove. Perhaps she would find poor Benjamin Foster hiding in the grove too. He was always being accused of something, and she feared she was about to be judged for something she couldn't control. Perhaps they could start their own settlement for scapegoats. They could welcome all of Good Springs' misunderstood, misinformed, and miscreants.

Gabe reached the pew, snapping Olivia from her fantasy of running away. Christopher scooted down for him to sit beside her. Gabe took her hand and didn't let go. He knew about the word blindness and hadn't rejected her. If he could boldly face the elders knowing Olivia's flaw might be exposed, she could too.

Teddy Cotter stood at the front of the room beside Mrs. Cotter. His sad eyes scanned the faces of the men he'd trusted since they all had planned their migration, fought the sea to survive, and settled the new land. He cleared his throat. "I understand you all know Cora has been accused of theft. They say she has been taking food from neighbors and milking their cows in the middle of the night." He glanced briefly at Olivia then pulled Mrs. Cotter close to his side as he continued. "It is not true. My wife works hard for our family. She can cook like a miracle worker, but that is no reason to accuse her of wrongdoing. If there is a thief among us, we must root him out. But my wife is no thief."

Reverend Colburn leaned against the side of the lectern and closed the cover of his Bible. "Thank you, Teddy. Unfortunately, several families have reported waking up to cows already milked. Yesterday morning my wife discovered an emptied shelf in our root cellar."

Mrs. Cotter's glare was fixed on the door at the back of the room. Her wiry hair stuck out around the edges of her brown bonnet. Her lips twitched intermittently, but she didn't say a word or look at Reverend Colburn.

The reverend nodded and motioned to the front row. "Olivia, Christopher, please stand."

Olivia's stomach dropped.

Reverend Colburn looked at Mr. Vestal. "Christopher, please tell the elders what you witnessed."

Christopher folded his hands calmly in front of his body. "When I realized someone was milking our cow, I started leaving the dog outside at night. Nights I did, we would have milk the next morning. My suspicion grew and just over a month ago I decided to lock the barn one night and watch to see who it was."

"And who did you see?" Reverend Colburn asked.

Christopher looked at Mrs. Cotter. "It was Cora. She came onto the property alone, holding a milk pail. She tried to get into my barn. There was a full moon that night, so I had a clear look at her face. Teddy, you know I would do anything for you and Cora. Susanna loved you both very much. I would have given you every drop of milk we had if you asked. Still would. I never wanted to testify against you, Cora, but I must tell the truth."

"And Christopher didn't witness this alone." Reverend Colburn said, looking at Olivia. "Miss Owens was with him that evening. Miss Owens, tell us what you saw."

Olivia swallowed hard and kept her focus on Reverend Colburn. "It was just as Mr. Vestal said. I'd stayed late at the Vestal house because we suspected the thief would come if he kept the dog inside. I saw Mrs. Cotter walk to the barn. She tried to get in, but it was locked, so she went to the chicken coop."

Mrs. Cotter snapped her gaze away from the door and pointed at Olivia. "She doesn't know what she saw!"

Mr. Cotter gently pulled his wife's pointing hand back down and asked her, "Did you go to the Vestals' barn at night?"

When Mrs. Cotter didn't answer her husband, he glanced nervously between her and the reverend. "Maybe she had a good reason to go to his barn. They didn't see her steal anything. Right, Cora?" His voice faltered as he scrambled to defend his wife. "Why did you go to the Vestals' barn? Perhaps you needed to borrow something and didn't want to wake them. Was that it?"

"It's her fault," she hissed and pointed again at Olivia. "She doesn't know what she saw because she has a demon—a monster that haunts her and keeps her from teaching our children properly."

Mr. Cotter's countenance fell. Reverend Colburn drew his head back in surprise. Mrs. Cotter's eyes widened and her volume rose. "That's right! Olivia Owens is tormented by a demon that blocks her vision. She told my Peggy all about it. Ask her yourself! Ask her!"

"That is enough, Cora," Teddy said, trying to calm his wife.

Reverend Colburn held up a hand, demanding silence. "Cora, have you been stealing food from the other families?"

Mrs. Cotter peeled her cruel gaze away from Olivia. "I have a family of nine. We will die here in this godforsaken land. There is nothing here. Nothing to eat. Not enough. We have to go home." Her shoulders slumped. "It's nonsense to build a schoolhouse as if we are going to live our lives here. We need to build a ship and go home."

The reverend angled his head a degree. "Cora, you are home. This land is our home now. And we have plenty to eat."

Mrs. Cotter flung her wrist to her forehead and began to weep with dramatic sobs.

Mr. Cotter drew her close. "Forgive her, gentlemen. And me. I am truly sorry. I didn't know, but I will make full restitution. Christopher, Olivia, I am sorry."

Compassion filled the reverend's voice. "Cora, you must not steal again."

She nodded and pulled a lace-trimmed handkerchief from her sleeve.

It wasn't the confession Olivia had hoped for, but it was a step back from lunacy. Everyone watched in silence, waiting for Mrs. Cotter's repentance. She wiped her tears, then squared her shoulders and eyed Olivia coldly. "You must be pleased with yourself. Look at you standing there full of haughty satisfaction! Did the evil spirit that controls your vision compel you to turn everyone against me?"

Teddy released his supportive grip. "Cora, don't."

Mrs. Cotter's dark eyes bore a hole through Olivia's heart. "A monster controls you. That's what you told my Peggy.

Didn't you? A monster hides words from you and that is why you cannot read." She looked past her husband at the reverend. "You are entrusting our children's education to a demon possessed teacher who cannot read."

Gabe shot to his feet. "She is not demon possessed. If anyone here has an evil spirit, it is you!"

"Enough!" Reverend Colburn removed his spectacles and rubbed one eye with the back of his hand. Silence fell upon the room as he laid his glasses on the lectern and drummed his fingers on his Bible. "Cora, your theft has caused division in our community. I understand the human desire to defend yourself by lying and denying the charge, but the truth is clear. In your heart you know what is right and what is good. We want you restored to this community, and that cannot happen until you repent."

Mrs. Cotter tried to point at Olivia again, but this time her husband caught her arm before she could raise it. She lifted her chin toward Olivia. "What about her? She has been fooling us all."

The reverend looked at Mrs. Cotter over the gold rim of his spectacles. "We will not consider your accusations unless you first confess your sin."

She lowered her chin a notch. "I took what my family needed. My Teddy works his fingers to the bone for this settlement, and I had to keep my family fed."

Mr. Cotter furrowed his brow at her. "Cora, we have plenty. God has provided abundantly for all of us."

"It never feels that way." Her shoulders began to shake. "I disappointed you, Teddy. Forgive me." Her tears returned, this time with sincerity. She panted between sobs and crumbled into the pew.

Mr. Cotter dabbed his wife's red face with his handkerchief and waved Doctor Ashton over. Whatever had made Mrs. Cotter fear for her family's survival had driven her to theft and had finally overcome her nerves. She hadn't been the same since they had endured the voyage. Though they had plenty, she had become stuck in an unnecessary fight for survival. They had all experienced the same journey and toil, but instead of it increasing her faith, she had given in to fear. And now it had suffocated her life.

Reverend Colburn closed his Bible. "Teddy, perhaps you should take her home."

Mr. Cotter nodded. He and Doctor Ashton helped Mrs. Cotter stand. They slowly walked one on either side of her, supporting her shaking body. She passed the first pew then stopped and turned back. "I have confessed my sin. Now please, for the sake of the children, test this girl. She shouldn't be teaching something she cannot do. She told my Peggy she cannot read. My Peggy doesn't lie."

Olivia's breath caught in her lungs. Peggy's lies had crippled her confidence as a young girl and almost ruined her relationship with Gabe. She opened her mouth to say as much but stopped her tongue when Reverend Colburn lifted his Bible from the lectern.

He held the book out to her. "Miss Owens, please read a passage so Mrs. Cotter can go home and rest."

Gabe leaned in. "You don't have to do this."

"Yes, I do," she said as she took it. She read the Bible's cover to herself. The letters were perfectly clear. She thumbed the Bible's pages in half and it fell open to the Psalms. She began reading the chapter on the right hand page. "Psalm One Hundred Thirty-nine. Lord, thou hast searched me, and known me." Confidence filled her voice as she easily read aloud. This was the voice she hoped to have in class Monday. "Thou knowest my downsitting and mine uprising, thou understandest my thought afar off..." She read another verse and another and felt Gabe relax beside her. She could see clearly all the way to the tenth verse and then the eleventh. It felt as if she were running at full speed, barely touching the ground. Maybe she'd been healed. Maybe she'd only needed to confess her affliction for it to go away. She had told Gabe, and he still loved her. Maybe that was her cure.

She boldly read verse twelve and even glanced up at the reverend between stanzas. Then as her eyes moved to the next line, verse thirteen disappeared. Only little scratch marks were left. They resembled bird prints in the sand more than letters on a page.

She closed her eyes and imagined the rest of words in that Psalm. When she opened them again, she recited the next verse from memory. "I will praise thee; for I am fearfully and wonderfully made: marvelous are thy works; and that my soul knoweth right well."

She was fearfully and wonderfully made.

The flaw God had allowed her to live with only made her stronger. It was the reason she wanted the children to have a good education. God had a purpose for her condition. She handed the Bible back to Reverend Colburn then rubbed her sweaty hands on her skirt.

"Thank you, Miss Owens. There," the reverend said to the elders, "Miss Owens can read just fine. Mrs. Cotter, you must drop this matter. Teddy, please remind your daughter that God doesn't tolerate lying and neither will we."

"Wait." Olivia couldn't hide the truth any longer. "Peggy didn't lie. Not this time anyway." All eyes were on Olivia, just as she'd always dreaded. She swallowed her fear. "I am able to read. I enjoy reading. I love to teach children to read. It wasn't easy for me to learn though because the words don't always appear for me. And yes, as I told Peggy, when I was a child I imagined a monster held its hand between my eyes and the page." She glanced at Doctor Ashton, who supportively nodded once. "The doctor assured me it was no such thing and that my vision was fine. I don't know what causes the words to disappear for me or when it will happen, so I memorize the lessons the night before I teach. I did read the first part of that Bible passage from the text. When I could no longer see the words, I spoke from memory." She looked at Reverend Colburn. "This doesn't mean I can't teach. It simply means I must work twice as hard as any other schoolteacher to prepare, just as I had to work twice as hard as the other children to learn when I was a student. But I did it. God has a purpose for this in my life. He gave me these eyes and this desire to teach."

No one spoke.

Gabe gently took her hand. A grin lit Doctor Ashton's face, puffing his bearded cheeks. Her father tilted his head, gazing at her with kind eyes.

Reverend Colburn slowly slid his Bible back onto the lectern. "Miss Owens, God gave you the strength to accomplish all that you have. We are blessed to have such a woman willing to teach our children." He gazed at each person in the room the way he did during his sermons. "We must all accept the circumstances God has given us. He has proven His faithfulness many times, and we are wrong to ever doubt Him. If we don't constantly acknowledge what God has done for us, we will allow fear to take hold. Each of us must rely on His strength through the challenges and use the talents He has given for His purpose—even when those talents come with difficulties."

CHAPTER TWENTY-ONE

Morning sunlight warmed the empty schoolhouse as Olivia opened the window shutters. Though still a month until the equinox, spring came early in the Land. It stirred a soft breeze from the nearby ocean that mixed with the scent of the classroom's fresh gray leaf lumber. She inhaled the heady aromas of home. There couldn't be a more pleasant morning for the first day teaching in the new schoolhouse.

The lessons were prepared, the desks in perfect rows, and the stack of textbooks ready to distribute. As she ambled around the classroom, she let her hand trail along the edge of the tables until she came to the desk Gabe had built her. It was long with drawers on either side. She opened the drawer on the right to re-read the secret message Gabe had carved in the drawer's wood: *G.M. + O.O.* She traced her finger along their joined initials.

Gabe tapped a knuckle on the open door at the opposite end of the classroom. "Excuse me, Miss Owens. Are you enrolling new students?"

"Why, yes I am." Olivia smiled and met him between the student desks and the door. "But you probably can't afford the tuition."

He hooked his thumbs in his pockets and lowered his chin. "Try me."

"Well, seeing as how you built the place, I suppose I could waive your fees."

"How very generous," he said, grinning.

She dropped the playful pretense. "Actually, I don't recall thanking you for building all this. It's far better than I could have hoped for. Thank you."

"You are most welcome." He glanced over his shoulder at the empty doorway. "My sister and brothers will be here soon, so I won't stay long. I saw the door open and had to come see you before everyone arrived." He drew her into his arms. "I'm proud of you. You have been faithful to your calling."

"Teaching is important to me. This is all I ever wanted."

He pulled back and looked down at her, taking both of her hands in his. "That isn't true. It sounds noble, but you want more."

He was right. More than teaching, she wanted to see words clearly every time see looked at a page, but that wasn't God's plan for her. She shrugged. "The word blindness will never go away, but I'm learning to trust God with it."

"I wasn't talking about that."

She cast her gaze around the classroom, out the open door to the village road, and then back to his handsome face. "What else do I want?"

"A family… a home…" The blue of his eyes brightened, matching the eternal sky outside the doorway. "You want me. I love you, Liv. I always have. It's time we joined our lives. Marry me."

Every drop of joy in her heart pumped through her veins. She entwined her fingers in his. "Yes, I will!"

He leaned down to kiss her and wrapped her in his arms, lifting her until her feet left the floor. When he set her down, she wove her fingers through the short hair behind his head, wanting to stay in his embrace. "I suppose I could miss the first day of school."

He chuckled. "No, not after all you've been through for this day." He reached into his coat pocket and pulled out a ring. "I'm going to finish the house this week, but I will be ready for you Sunday. We could get married after church... unless you need more time."

"No, I'm ready."

"I thought so." Grinning wildly, he slid the ring onto her finger. "This was my grandmother's."

Three rubies were embedded in the gold band. They caught the light and cast flecks of red across her skin. "It is beautiful," she whispered.

"Just like you." He lifted her chin with a finger. "Your worth is far above rubies. I will never let you forget that." He kissed her once more with brief and poignant passion. "I will see you Sunday."

"Sunday," she repeated on a breath as he strode away.

She paced to the door and leaned against the frame as she watched him disappear down the path to his house... soon to be their house. They would spend their lives together, him building the settlement and her teaching the next generation.

She only had a moment to absorb the warmth of the morning sun and the sweetness of being engaged to the man she loved.

Students began coming down the road from both directions. She checked her silver watch pin. It was time. She reached to a rope that hung beside the stoop and pulled, ringing the bell.

Mrs. Colburn pushed her baby carriage, walking her children from their home on the south end of the village, and Peggy escorted the Cotter children from the north. As Peggy hurried the children along, Olivia ducked inside the classroom. She put a hand against the wall. "Lord, please let the Colburns arrive first."

Little Jane Cotter's voice sounded from just beyond the yard. "Miss Owens! Miss Owens!"

Olivia smoothed her dress and stepped back into the doorway. "Hello, Jane. Good morning, Conrad. Come in and hang your coats on the rack." She glanced at Peggy, who stood at the bottom of the steps. "Thank you for bringing them today. I'm sure they can find their own way tomorrow."

"I deserve that, I suppose." Peggy looked down at her hands. "Listen, Olivia, I really am sorry for what I did." She fidgeted with her lace cuffs. "You worked hard and I tried to ruin it—with the school and with Gabe. I never should have told my mother about your... condition. She hasn't been right after the voyage, but she's been trying to change since everything that happened last week. Anyway, I am sorry... for everything."

Olivia checked the road. The Colburns were fast approaching. Marian walked behind them with Benjamin, and the Vestal children were coming from the other direction. She wanted this conversation to end. She flicked a glance at Peggy. "It's fine."

Peggy ascended the first step. "No, it is not fine. I miss your friendship. You were my only true friend here, and I let you down. Please, forgive me. I want us to go back to how we used to be."

Olivia stopped watching the others and studied Peggy. Her long face and sad eyes bespoke sincerity.

Olivia wanted the whole ordeal behind her. She waved a hand, dismissively. "Everyone makes mistakes. You probably got jealous or were overwhelmed by your mother's behavior or were bored—"

Peggy took another step up. "Don't excuse my behavior. That is not forgiving anything. I treated you badly. I'm not asking you to justify it, but to forgive me."

Olivia drew her head back. It had been so long since she had heard Peggy say anything wise that she'd forgotten she was capable of it. "Then I won't try to figure out why you behaved the way you did. I'll simply forgive you."

"And give me another chance?"

"Of course." She reached out and squeezed Peggy's gloved hand.

Peggy's gaze landed on the gold and ruby ring. She sucked in a breath and released a happy squeal. "Oh, Olivia! It's beautiful!"

"He asked me this morning."

"When will you be married?

"Sunday after church," she answered as the Colburns arrived. She gave Peggy a quick hug. "You will be there, won't you?"

Peggy nodded. "Of course."

After Olivia welcomed the Colburn children, Marian arrived with Benjamin. She cradled baby Frederick with one arm and held a rolled up paper in the other hand. "Help me open this, Ben," she said as she handed the paper to her brother.

Benjamin flipped his shaggy hair off his forehead and unrolled the paper, revealing a world map.

Marian explained, "It's for your classroom wall from Jonah. He said it is not to remind everyone of where we cannot go, but how far God has brought us."

"It's perfect," Olivia said as Benjamin rolled it back up. "Thank you. Please give Jonah my thanks as well."

Marian switched the baby to the other arm. "You deserve to have it after the way you've inspired the village. Speaking of which, Ben has something to ask you."

Olivia gave Benjamin her attention. "What is it?"

He handed her the rolled up map then brushed his fingertips together. "I heard about the trouble you have seeing words sometimes, and maybe when that happens, I could read for you."

"Are you saying you would like to attend school?"

He slid his hands into his pockets. "If it's all right with you."

"Of course. I would love to have you in class."

"When I heard you might need help sometimes, I thought maybe I could try... for a while... until later in the spring anyway because then I'll have more chores."

Marian smiled at Olivia. "What do you think?"

"That sounds wonderful!" Happy tears welled up in the corners of Olivia's eyes. She blinked them back. "And again, we're all very sorry you were blamed for the fire at the chapel. Mrs. Cotter admitted to the reverend that she started it, hoping to stop school."

Benjamin crossed his arms, pressed his lips together, and nodded in the way the older men did when they were solemnly pleased. "I'm glad you didn't let her stop you from teaching, Miss Owens."

"Thank you, Benjamin." She pointed Benjamin into the classroom. After he went inside, she turned back to Marian. "He has come a long way."

"We all have."

"Including me." Olivia held up her hand to show the ring.

Marian beamed. "It looks beautiful on you."

"You knew?"

"Of course," Marian shrugged. "Gabe is my husband's closest friend. I know about everything." She winked after she dragged out the word.

Olivia mocked a groan and they laughed together.

More families arrived, bringing children to the schoolhouse on the sandy lot. Doctor Ashton came with Sarah and James, Mrs. Roberts brought two of her daughters, and Hannah Vestal carried a lunch pail as she escorted Doris and Wade. Everyone wanted a look inside the new classroom before they left the students for the day. Olivia proudly welcomed them in.

Lastly, her mother arrived with Alice, Almeda, Martha, and Richie. She wished her father would have come too, but only because she wanted to show him what she'd accomplished.

Mary nudged Richie as he climbed the steps. "Behave yourself, young man." She gave Olivia a look. "Richie knows he is here on probation. He's still upset with himself for cutting your braid. Your father said if he doesn't behave, you are to correct him forcefully on the spot or send him home."

Olivia nodded, hoping that wouldn't be necessary on their first day in the schoolhouse.

Mary whispered. "Do you need me to stay?"

"No, I am ready for this. All three of my monitors are here, and even Benjamin Foster has offered to read for me when I can't see the words."

"Benjamin? That's wonderful. I hope all of your monitors are as helpful to you as you were to me. I'm proud of you, and your father is too." Mary smiled and patted her hand then she looked at the ring. "Oh good, Gabe came to see you."

"You knew about his plans too?"

"I have known since he asked your father's blessing during the autumn. Pretty ring. Your father never gave me a ring, but Gabe is quite the romantic, isn't he?"

Olivia looked at the rubies as they sparkled in the light. "There is more to Gabriel McIntosh than I ever imagined."

As the children settled into their seats, Olivia walked back to the doorway and took one last look outside. From the chapel to the cabins and the road that led to the homes beyond the little village, this settlement was home. As peace settled in her heart, she gazed up at the clear blue sky. "Thank you, Lord, for entrusting me with these children. Let my words speak Your wisdom and may Your strength sustain me."

Thank you for reading my book. I'm so glad you went on this journey with me. More Uncharted stories await you! Are you ready for the adventure?

I know it's important for you to enjoy these wholesome, inspirational stories in your favorite format, so I've made sure all of my books are available in ebook, paperback, and large print versions.

Below is a quick description of each story so that you can determine which books to order next...

The Uncharted Series
A hidden land settled by peaceful people ~ The first outsider in 160 years

The Land Uncharted (#1)
Lydia's secluded society is at risk when an injured fighter pilot's parachute carries him to her hidden land.

Uncharted Redemption (#2)
When vivacious Mandy is forced to depend on strong, silent Levi, she must learn to accept tender love from the one man who truly knows her.

Uncharted Inheritance (#3)
Bethany and Everett belong together, but when a mysterious man arrives in the Land, everything changes.

Christmas with the Colburns (#4)
When Lydia faces a gloomy holiday in the Colburn house, an unexpected gift brightens her favorite season.

Uncharted Hope (#5)
While Sophia and Nicholas wrestle with love and faith, a stunning discovery outside the Land changes everything.

Uncharted Journey (#6)
When horse trainer Solo moves to Falls Creek, widow Eva gets a second chance at love. Meanwhile, Bailey's quest to reach the Land costs her everything.

Uncharted Destiny (#7)
The Uncharted story continues when Bailey and Revel face an impossible rescue mission in the Land's treacherous mountains.

Uncharted Promises (#8)
When Sybil and Isaac get snowed in, it takes more than warm meals and cozy fireplaces to help them find love at the Inn at Falls Creek.

Uncharted Freedom (#9)
When Naomi takes the housekeeping job at The Inn at Falls Creek to hide from one past, another finds her.

Uncharted Courage (#10)
With the survival of the Land at stake and their hearts on the line, Bailey and Revel must find the courage to love.

The Uncharted Beginnings Series
Embark on an unforgettable 1860s journey with the Founders as they discover the Land.

Aboard Providence (#1)
When Marian and Jonah's ship gets marooned on a mysterious uncharted island, they must build a settlement to survive. Love and adventure await!

Above Rubies (#2)

When schoolteacher Olivia needs the settlement elders' approval, she must hide her dyslexia from everyone, even charming carpenter Gabe.

All Things Beautiful (#3)
Henry is the last person Hannah wants reading her story... and the first person to awaken her heart.

Find out more on my website keelybrookekeith.com or feel free to email me at keely@keelykeith.com where I answer every message personally.

See you in the Land!
Keely

ABOUT THE AUTHOR

Keely Brooke Keith writes inspirational frontier-style fiction with a futuristic twist, including *The Land Uncharted* (Shelf Unbound Notable Romance 2015) and *Aboard Providence* (2017 INSPY Awards Longlist).

Born in St. Joseph, Missouri, Keely was a tree-climbing, baseball-loving 80s kid. She grew up in a family who moved often, which fueled her dreams of faraway lands. When she isn't writing, Keely enjoys teaching home school lessons and playing bass guitar. Keely, her husband, and their daughter live on a hilltop south of Nashville, Tennessee.

CPSIA information can be obtained
at www.ICGtesting.com
Printed in the USA
FSHW012019030122
87376FS